The Long Trail Back

Also by Todhunter Ballard in Large Print:

Loco and the Wolf
Roundup
West of Quarantine

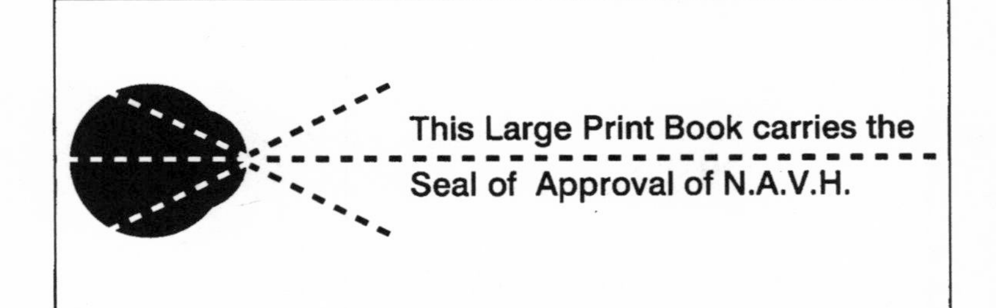

The Long Trail Back

Todhunter Ballard

ER
NG

Published in 2004 by arrangement with
Golden West Literary Agency.

Wheeler Large Print Western.

The text of this Large Print edition is unabridged.
Other aspects of the book may vary from the original edition.

Set in 16 pt. Plantin by Al Chase.

Printed in the United States on permanent paper.

ISBN 1-58724-646-5 (lg. print : sc : alk. paper)

The Long Trail Back

National Association for Visually Handicapped
serving the partially seeing

As the Founder/CEO of NAVH, the only national health agency solely devoted to those who, although not totally blind, have an eye disease which could lead to serious visual impairment, I am pleased to recognize Thorndike Press* as one of the leading publishers in the large print field.

Founded in 1954 in San Francisco to prepare large print textbooks for partially seeing children, NAVH became the pioneer and standard setting agency in the preparation of large type.

Today, those publishers who meet our standards carry the prestigious "Seal of Approval" indicating high quality large print. We are delighted that Thorndike Press is one of the publishers whose titles meet these standards. We are also pleased to recognize the significant contribution Thorndike Press is making in this important and growing field.

Lorraine H. Marchi, L.H.D.
Founder/CEO
NAVH

* Thorndike Press encompasses the following imprints: Thorndike, Wheeler, Walker and Large Print Press.

ONE

Eight men; gaunt, trail sore, half-famished, they rode with the silent perseverance which had carried them through two thousand miles of unfriendly country.

Long ago they had ceased useless conversation, for even the forming of words burned energy and energy they no longer had.

From the head of the straggling single line Carstairs looked back to see that no one had fallen out in sheer exhaustion. The horse under him stopped, sensing that its rider was no longer pushing, and the animals behind it halted uncertainly as if not quite believing their good fortune.

For the horses were nearly as beat as the men who rode them. True, they had eaten with more regularity, but the grass in the country through which they had traveled was short, and the water scarce.

Joe Blunt, his barrel-like body appearing deflated, pushed his limping horse forward until his stirrup brushed that of Carstairs.

"How much further, Captain?"

Reese Carstairs did not know. He scraped the lean cut of his bearded jaw with the heel of his thumb.

"Can't be much beyond this ridge, if I figure right. I could sure use some of that beef right now. Hope that man in Santa Fe knew what he was talking about."

He turned in his saddle, looking again at the men who followed him, and out of habit raised a fist, making the swinging gesture for advance.

"Ho."

They did not charge, but the line came into motion, laboring up the trail that climbed in slanting planes connected by sharp switchbacks, upward through the pole-pine timber toward the crest.

They made it at noon, and Joe Blunt saw the doe as he lurched up into the crotch of the narrow pass. She stood within the edge of the timber, gazing down at them curiously.

The rifle's crack echoed in the deepness of the pass, bounding back and forth between the rocky face hemming them in on the north and south, until it seemed multiplied a thousandfold, as if all of Kirby Smith's men of the Trans-Mississippi army had fired at once.

The bullet caught the doe in the neck, knocking her flat with the solid impact, and almost before she had hit the ground Carstairs was upon her, driving his horse forward, pulling the heavy Colts in case she were still alive.

He need not have worried. The slug had broken her neck. He swung down, drawing the wide-bladed, unsheathed knife from his belt and skinning her out while the blood ran, still warm, across his hands.

The carcass he slung over his saddle, and his horse was so beat that not even the strange burden or the smell of fresh blood spooked it.

Carstairs led the way then on foot as the trail turned downward. Within a thousand feet it reached a creek which dropped in a silver spray over the sheer rock to the right.

Here they built their fire and set the meat to cook, some of them eating it half-raw because the press of hunger was so great.

There was no salt, no bread, no coffee, and they needed none. The liver Carstairs prepared with more care, laying it out on a flat rock and slicing it into thin strips which he distributed to be roasted on pointed sticks above the glowing coals.

When they were finished nothing remained save the picked bones and the two haunches. These Carstairs wrapped in a blanket against the flies and tied across his saddlebow.

They rested, and rose again and continued down the west side of the ridge, finally breaking out of the heavy timber to a rim, and from there had a view of the valley spreading beneath them.

Carstairs caught his breath. In his fondest imaginings he had not pictured a place like this. He could not tell the valley's length, for it ran out farther than the eye could see, even in the sharp clearness of the mountain air.

The width he judged at thirty to forty miles, bordered east and west by tree-skirted slopes rising up beyond timberline so that their bare tops gleamed white in the glare of the afternoon sun.

The valley floor was a thick carpet of heavy green, laced by half a dozen streams, from this distance thin, curving snakes wriggling their way through the deep coat of standing grass.

"Man." It was Joe Blunt, pulling up at his side. "That's something, ain't it? Something to look at and dream about. You think this is the place?"

"Got to be." Reese Carstairs was as convinced as if he had already seen his brother. "Man in Denver city described it, remember. Said it was the greatest pasture in the world. Well, you're looking at that."

He put his horse in motion and the animal, seeming also to see the promise of the valley floor, stepped out livelier than he had done in weeks, his head up, his ears erect, like a colt again.

It took a full hour to drop to the bench, to

follow the trail looping through the lessening clumps of timber, until all around them was nothing but grass.

They rode around a small hill that jutted from the rolling floor and saw the town. It lay a good five miles away, its scattered buildings looking no more than matchboxes in the distance, and a ragged rebel yell went up from the line of men, a yell of relief and hope, of returning belief in a future they had long since written off.

They were again Carstairs' Raiders, with the fierce pride in themselves, the sure confidence in their ability and in their cause which had made them the scourge of the Union armies west of the Mississippi.

They came into the outskirts just at dusk, and if they were disappointed by the lack of size they hid their disappointment well.

Walden lay on a gentle rise above a curving street, its buildings solid and weather-tight, squared logs chinked with white mud against a climate which sometimes produced temperatures of forty below; a cow town; a trading town catering to the trappers who still roamed the streams of the Medicine Bows; a mining town supplying a dozen properties, for bordering the valley was some of the most mineralized strata in the West.

There was one main street, the trail itself, and even along it the stores did not present an even front since each builder had placed his structure as he chose, without regard to maintaining setbacks or lining up with his neighbors.

Behind these rows other men had built their homes and business buildings on winding paths, even in the middle of huge grass plots.

They came in slowly, silent now, the enthusiasm invoked by their first sight of the place washed away, inundated by their fatigue.

The biggest building was Kobbler's Store. It sat midway in the second block, behind a high gallery of sunburned boards that served as both a loafing place and a loading dock to which the ranchers and mining men could back their high-wheeled wagons.

Next to it was the town's largest saloon, and beyond that a two-storied log building carrying the sign HOTEL above its door.

Carstairs swung his horse in to the rail at the side of the store building and stepped down stiffly, turning slowly to study with sharp curiosity the town he had ridden so many weary miles to find, and which he fully believed would be his home.

His men followed him, stretching their saddle-stiffened muscles, silent, watchful, their eyes above the lines of their ragged beards more like the eyes of animals than of men.

Unconsciously they drew together into a close group after they fastened their horses.

For nearly ten years they had drawn together thus for mutual protection, surrounded as they had constantly been by enemies.

Only Carstairs did not join them. He ducked under the rail and climbed the steps bridging the corner of the gallery with the dust which was the road.

There were a dozen loafers on the wide porch, riders in their stained, tight pants, townsmen in shirt sleeves with fancy arm bands and hard derbies.

He felt the curiosity of their attention and was very conscious of his patched clothes, his broken hat, his bearded cheeks, but he purposely refused to meet their stares. Instead he reached the double storm doors now standing wide and stepped into the huge dim room beyond.

The dimness was caused by the smallness of the windows; little better than loopholes in the thick log walls, and the fact that what little light these slits permitted to enter was partly blocked by the heaps of merchandise which literally choked the place.

Carstairs stopped, looking around, feasting his eyes on this display of wealth. Years of war and eight years in the poverty of Mexico had almost made him forget that somewhere in the world there were enough clothes, enough blankets, enough food that all might be satisfied.

There were only three customers in the

store, lined at the low rear counter, and only one clerk to serve their wants.

He was a short man, with shoulders almost as broad as Joe Blunt's. His head was bald except for a fringe around the crown of brownish, discouraged, struggling hair. He wore a white shirt, the cuffs covered by sateen wristlets, a string bow tie and a horseshoe-shaped diamond stickpin in the front of his shirt.

He glanced appraisingly at Carstairs, sizing him up from his ragged appearance and unkempt hair as a saddle tramp, and wondering what excuse he would think up to refuse the handout for which this man would undoubtedly ask.

He served one customer, then another, and finally the third, purposely taking as long with each transaction as was possible. When at last the store was empty save for himself and Carstairs he turned reluctantly, exposing an eyetooth made of gold as he asked,

"Help you?"

"You can tell me the way to my brother's ranch."

The request caught Moose Kobbler by surprise. He was at heart a kindly man, to which many uncollected items on his books bore mute testimony.

"What's his name?"

"Alf Carstairs."

Moose Kobbler would not have been more amazed if this ragged man had claimed relationship with the President of the United States, for the Carstairs ranch was the biggest outfit in the valley.

"North," he said. "The headquarters buildings are about fifteen miles from town, the ranch runs clear past Cowdry to the north end."

"Just follow the trail?"

"Sure. Say" — he had just thought of something — "your brother's wife is in the back room, picking out some goods."

"Wife?" Reese Carstairs was startled. He did not know that Alf had married, but then, he had not heard from Alf directly in nearly five years.

"May I see her?"

"Come on." Kobbler led the way into the rear room.

Here dress goods, curtains, blankets, and spreads were stacked on shelves against the wall, and a woman in a riding skirt was examining one bolt of cloth after another.

"Mrs. Carstairs." It was Kobbler. "Here's a man who would like to talk to you."

She turned slowly, still fingering the end of cloth.

Reese Carstairs stared at her, unbelieving.

"Nell."

For a full minute she did not know him. Then her face went white, the cloth slipped from her fingers.

"Reese? Reese."

She was running toward him. She was in his arms, her head against his shoulder, his bearded cheek against her hair.

"Reese, Reese! My God! You're dead! You're dead!"

TWO

The shock of seeing Nell Borden made it difficult for Reese Carstairs to think clearly for a moment. He bent his head and his hungry lips found hers and held there until she pushed him away with a little gesture of desperation.

"Reese, no. Please."

He straightened then, and from the corner of his eye caught a glimpse of Moose Kobbler standing in the doorway gawking at them, and the clerk's words rushed back through his consciousness.

"Mrs. Carstairs . . . Mrs. Carstairs."

There had to be some mistake. This was Nell Borden, the girl he himself was going to marry.

He saw the glint of sharp interest in the clerk's eye and his voice was hard, sharp, flat.

"Get out of here."

Reese Carstairs had been seventeen when he rode out to war, eighteen when he led his first company in its charge at the Second Battle of Bull Run. The habit of command was strong and it carried in his words now, and sent the bald-headed clerk scurrying like a frightened rabbit for the shelter of his counter.

The girl put a quick hand on Carstairs' arm.

"You shouldn't have done that. I know him. The story will be all over town in an hour."

"What story?" He turned back to her. There was an air of unreality about this whole thing, as if his brain had finally cracked under the tortures he had endured, as if he were walking through a murky nightmare.

"That I kissed you. That you held me in your arms."

"But you're mine. It's not the first time I've kissed you."

"That," she said, and there was no steadiness in her voice, "was a long time ago."

He was trying to understand, trying to grasp what had happened to him, to them. Only a few minutes ago he had ridden into this town with full confidence that the future was assured, that after all the years of war and prison he could settle down to running his ranch, could send to Texas for this girl and that they could mend their shattered lives.

"You said you'd wait."

She was crying, not loudly, not with hysteria, but with a deep, consuming grief.

"What was there to wait for? You were dead. The future was dead, the world we knew was dead. Reese, you simply must understand. Texas was an open grave with Yankee carpetbaggers picking at the corpse. God in heaven, you have no idea of the misery."

He thought about the Mexican prison, the firing squads after Maximilian fell, the ranch deep in the tropic belt where they labored in a plight far worse than the peons around them. Yes, he had known misery too, and hopelessness. He should understand, but somehow he did not. All he knew was that the girl he wanted was married to his brother.

"What made you think I was dead?"

"A man came out of Mexico, four years ago. He brought word to Alf that you had been executed by a firing squad for trying to escape. Alf wrote me then. He said the ranch was established, the houses were built. He offered to bring my whole family north, out of the wreckage of Texas, if I would marry him."

"I see." He didn't see. He said, "Nell, this is wrong and you know it. We were going to be married almost from the time we could both talk. We'll have to go to Alf and explain. We'll have to make him see that you must have a divorce."

She caught a sharp breath. "No."

"Yes," he said. "Yes." He had her by the shoulders, unconscious of the power of his hands, the way his thin fingers were biting into her soft flesh. "It's the only way, the honest way. You don't think I can have you around, seeing you day after day at the ranch, and keep my hands off you?"

"Reese," she pulled away. "Reese, I have two children."

"Children?" The idea had not even occurred to him. "Alf's children?"

"Who else's?"

"Oh, my God."

He buried his bearded face in his hands. He could feel the hot tears behind his eyes, but he did not cry. All through the years he had never cried save once, the day General Kirby Smith had surrendered, the last Confederate force to lay down its arms.

He had cried then, out of frustration and hatred and bitterness, but he had not surrendered. He had led his men across the river, offering his sword to the Mexican emperor, asking in return only the privilege of establishing a new South, a place where men like himself could build a new life.

And he had given his loyalty to the emperor, refusing to run when the French troops were withdrawn, when it became obvious that the native forces were deserting in droves.

He had stayed, and thirty of his Raiders had stayed with him. But he had sent his younger brother out with those who wanted to leave, racing for the safety of the border, preferring to take their chances in the reconstructed States rather than face the almost certain death by a revolutionary firing squad.

It was the last time he had seen Alf, and he remembered him as he had been then, tall, dark haired, slender, standing beside his horse on the red-baked mud of the garrison parade ground.

"You'd better come too," his brother had told him. "The show here is over."

He had realized that, but there was within him a stubborn streak which refused to down as long as any hope remained.

"You go," he said. "Here's a bill of sale for the ranch and the cattle, in your name. From what I hear there's a market for beef in the North. Take them there, but don't sell the breeding stock. Start a new outfit as far from Texas as you can get. When this is over I'll come and we'll build the ranch together."

They had shaken hands then, and he had given Alf his letter to Nell Borden. He had expected to see her within a few weeks, a few months at most, not five long years later.

He straightened now, not knowing whether moments or hours had elapsed, and found her watching him, the tears still beading her long eyelashes.

"What are you going to do?"

"Do?" He didn't know. He had given no thought to the future since her last words. What future? Why had he fought all these weary, cruel years to live? What was there to live for? "Go to the ranch, I guess. How is it?"

"Why, fine," she said, and a new note crept into her voice. "You never saw such feed, and even though the winters are terrible, the cattle ride through them to come out butter-fat in the spring."

"And Alf?" He realized with a start that he had not even asked about his brother's health.

"All right." There was an undernote of uncertainty in the words that made him look at her sharply.

"He's treating you all right, isn't he?"

"Yes. Oh, yes."

"How come you're in town alone? It's nearly dark."

"They're very busy, and there is some trouble. A man named Creed."

"What kind of trouble?"

She said slowly, "Rustling, a few shootings. Our men ride only in pairs."

"Yet they let you come to town alone?"

She gave him a faint smile. "Even Creed doesn't fight women."

He accepted this. "What did you bring, a buggy?"

"Buckboard. I'm afraid our roads weren't made for the fancier things."

"I'll take you home."

He was himself again, submerging his emotions as he had so often done in the past, becoming once more the taciturn man who kept his own counsel, neither asking nor giving advice.

The loafers still occupied the gallery, and Moose Kobbler had joined them. From their interested glances Carstairs guessed that Kobbler had already spread the story of the kiss, but he gave no indication that he saw. It was pointless to fight with these men. Let them think what they would.

He helped Nell Borden down the steps to where his Raiders waited in their tight, silent group, patient yet weary as dogs.

"This is my brother's wife." He spoke a little loudly to assure that the words carried to those on the gallery. "I'm going to ride out to the ranch with her in the buckboard. Joe, you lead my horse. The rest of you follow."

He turned to her as the men moved to free their horses and mount. Her eyes widened.

"Who are they?"

"What's left of Carstairs' Raiders."

"And you mean to keep them at the ranch?"

He was surprised. "Of course. We've been together for a long while."

"But we have a full crew, carefully picked men. I'm not sure Alf will want to put on so many."

Suddenly the reserve with which he had walled himself slipped, and a note almost harsh rose in his voice.

"I think you're wrong. Alf rode with these men once himself. Whether or not he likes it, they stay. Let's not forget that the ranch is mine."

She started visibly. "Yours?"

"Certainly. The cattle were mine, the ranch in Texas was mine, left to me by my mother's father. Remember that Alf and I are only half brothers."

She spoke in a careful tone. "I know that."

"But what are we talking about? Alf understands as well as I do that the only reason I gave him the bill of sale was to make it easier for him to drive the herd north."

She said slowly, "I'm not sure he does."

"It couldn't be any other way. Where's your rig?"

"At the livery."

They walked the street together, the late mountain light holding faintly although the sun had been down behind the western rim for nearly an hour, and came into the wide runway of the livery barn.

The girl spoke to the hostler and he went for her team. Then she removed her hat, exposing the braided black of her hair.

Looking at her in the lantern light Carstairs was sure that she was the most beautiful woman in the world. She was tall for a girl, her five feet six inches bringing her almost to his shoulder, and he knew a sudden driving impulse to draw her into his arms, to hold her so forever.

Even with the knowledge that she had borne his brother's children he felt the deep sense of possession. Since boyhood he had considered that she belonged to him, and it was something not easy to be rid of.

The hostler brought out the harnessed team. Carstairs helped to fasten the traces to the doubletree. Then he gave Nell a hand and watched the quick, lithe way she stepped up to the seat. He climbed beside her and turned the team northward.

His men waiting outside the barn fell in behind the light rig. Their horses, refreshed by the half hour of rest, stepped out with a little show of energy.

The darkness came with the suddenness of a dropping veil. One moment he could see every house in town as they passed, in the next it was hard to see the trail beyond the team.

He drove steadily but not hurriedly, mindful that the horses trailing them had come a long way. The team was young, only half-broken, with a desire to run which he curbed under a tight rein.

It occupied his full attention for the first few miles, and of this he was glad, for now that the first shock of meeting had passed he felt a certain constraint with the woman at his side.

It was strange. They had known each other so thoroughly since childhood and now he sensed that he did not know her at all, that the understanding between them was entirely gone. Nothing remained but the intensity of his yearning and dreams, for it had been those dreams which sustained him during the years, through the prison at Veracruz, then through the convict ranch where he had labored.

The moon rose slowly, first as a glow in the sky behind the eastern rim of the mountains and later as a yellow disk incredibly large and close in the clear, high country air.

He glanced at the woman, conscious that they had ridden a full ten miles without a word uttered between them.

Her eyes were forward, her right elbow on her knee, her chin cupped in her hand. She might have been asleep, but some sense told him that she was not.

"You said Alf brought your family up from Texas. Are they living at the ranch?"

She spoke without turning, and there was no interest in her voice.

"No. They've got a place up in the mouth of Kings Canyon."

He had no idea where Kings Canyon was and he did not pursue the subject. As the moon climbed the immense arch of the sky the light grew until the whole valley took on a soft, mysterious hue, and finally as they breasted a long swell he saw far off to the left the pinpoint glint of lights.

"The ranch?"

"The ranch."

The gate was two upright, peeled pole pines with a headboard between them, and burned deeply on the board was the Triple X of his grandfather's brand. His own brand.

It gave him a strange feeling as they drove under the headboard and followed the winding lane back toward the buildings set upon their rise against the western bench of the valley floor.

This was not the homecoming he had visualized. All the pleasure and anticipation were wiped away. And it was odd to be riding into a ranch which was his yet which he had never seen.

The whipcrack of the rifle yanked him erect on the hard seat.

His first thought was that they had been mistaken for someone else, that they were being attacked. He jerked up the team and snapped a glance behind him. His straggling, exhausted men were already in action, hauling their rifles from the worn boots.

These men knew war and killing and hardship and they reacted instantly. Not waiting for orders they fanned into a skirmish line before a half-dozen shots rattled from the distant group of buildings.

The firing, then, was not directed at themselves.

"Creed." Fear was raw in Nell Carstairs' voice. "With the crew away they'll burn the ranch."

Reese was already shoving the reins into her gloved hands.

"How many at home?"

"The cook. That's all."

He dived for the ground, waving at Blunt to bring up his horse.

"Stay here," he called to the girl.

"My babies."

He had forgotten that she had children. His voice was flat, driving.

"We'll get them. You stay here."

He grasped his horse's bridle and flung himself up, his orders terse, tight.

"Spread out. Come at them in a circle. Make them think we're a whole damn army. Make as much noise as you can."

Blunt's eyes had swept the scene ahead. His tone was disapproving.

"They'll only run. We could circle, hit the timber and maybe come on them before they know we're here."

"I want them to know. I want them to run. There are two kids in that house. The more bullets flying around the more chance they'll get hit."

He raised the hand which held his rifle and his voice cut out through the moonlit night with the old ring of authority that had flung them into a hundred headlong charges.

"Ho! Get the bastards!"

The line swept forward, the last eight men of Carstairs' Raiders. Reese knew a sudden surge of power such as he had not experienced in years, a pulse of strength, of self-certainty he had believed beaten out of him.

The firing ahead was steady now, and he saw that it was directed at the ranch house itself, and that only a single rifle answered. Apparently the attackers, intent upon the raid, had not yet spotted them. He saw a sudden flare of flame off to the side where someone fired a haystack.

He was much too distant for an effective shot but he brought his rifle to his shoulder, shooting, yelling, spurring his horse forward as fast as its tired legs would carry it.

His men took up the cry and the long-unheard rebel yell swelled eerily across the half-light of the Colorado plain.

They were seen. Some of the attackers swung and he saw the bright flash of their guns. He swept on, heedless that now he was within range, heedless that bullets kicked spits of dust from the hard ground beneath his horse's flying feet.

He fired again and yet again, and was conscious of his men galloping on either side, firing, yelling, making more noise than a full-strength Comanche war party.

The attackers broke. Reese could not be sure how many there were but he guessed not more than six or seven. Suddenly they reared their horses around and raced for the shelter of the bench timber close behind the yard.

The last man stopped to fire a second haystack, then drove after his fellows. Joe Blunt was only a hundred yards away. He dropped the fleeing figure with a careful shot and saw the dark form roll twice under the momentum of the heavy slug, then lie still.

His companions did not stop, but vanished into the gloom of the trees and for a moment the yard was a vacuum of silence after the tumult.

Then as Carstairs' men rode warily into the sun-baked space between the flanking buildings a gun flashed in the timber, Reese's foremost rider threw his arms wide and pitched out of his saddle, a formless yell wrenched from his dying throat.

A second shot knocked down a horse, hurling Whitey Ellis a dozen feet through the air to crash in a tumbled heap against the poles of the corral fence.

Reese shouted his order and watched his six remaining Raiders scatter, driving for shelter behind the buildings, swinging out of their saddles, letting the horses run on, bringing their rifles into play to rake the wall of brush from which the shots were coming.

Reese himself raced for a corner of the house and dropped to the ground in its deep shadow. Behind him he suddenly heard the running beat of the buckboard team, the high keen of the iron-rimmed wheels, and Nell Carstairs whipped them frantically into the moon-bathed yard.

A bullet struck her off horse in the neck. It reared and screamed in dying agony, shearing the pole, and fell backward clawing air and writhing. Its carcass toppled heavily on the dashboard of the light wagon, crushing it, smashing the right front wheel. The buckboard tilted crazily and Carstairs saw the girl thrown free, saw her land jarringly in the exposure of the open yard.

He had no way of knowing if she were alive or dead. He dropped his gun and, ignoring the bullets which whipped toward him from the dark trees a hundred yards beyond, ran from his shelter to crouch at her side.

One bullet tore at his hat, flinging it away. Another ripped through the shoulder of his patched coat without gashing his skin.

He had no consciousness of them, of anything save the girl. He slid his hands beneath her and lifted her and rose from his knees in one single movement. Then he was running again for the house, bent low and weaving to minimize the target he and his burden made, while his men sprayed shots from all angles to cover his passage.

He made it safely, bounding up the steps and across the gallery, almost running down a short, thick, red-faced man who stood frozen by surprise in the doorway.

The man had a nearly bald head and ears which stuck out from the sides of his naked head like flaps, and his powerful hands held a rifle across the stained kitchen apron covering his middle.

"Where will I put her?"

The cook jumped back at Reese's flung words, turning to scuttle down the central hall, to snatch a lamp from a wall bracket and swing in at the first door. Carstairs was only a step behind him. The room they entered was a parlor, and Carstairs laid the girl gently on the horsehair sofa.

The light showed the smear of dirt and scratched skin where her cheek had scraped the ground in her fall, the trickle of blood from the small cut above her lip.

Reese Carstairs was testing her legs, her arms, for possible breaks when a baby began to cry somewhere in the rear of the house.

As if on signal, Nell's eyes opened. She saw Reese, saw the cook behind him holding the lamp in one hand, his rifle in the other. She heard the crying and struggled to sit up.

"The babies, Pete? The babies?"

"All right, ma'am." The cook had a heavy voice with a trace of Irish brogue still lingering. "The shooting waked the little one, that's all."

"And Creed, did he come in the house?"

Pete shook his head. "I was out on the porch for a smoke when they rode up. I thought it was some of our crew coming back, but one of the jaspers threw a shot at me and I ducked for the door and grabbed the rifle."

She moved to stand up and winced. Reese stepped forward.

"Easy."

"It's nothing." She made it to her feet. "I think I twisted my knee. I'm all right." She started toward the children's room.

Reese watched her leave, then said to the cook, "Take care of her," and ran to the hall and down it to the front door.

Joe Blunt now held one corner of the house and Reese was relieved to see Whitey Ellis at the other. He had been afraid that the boy had been killed by the fall from his horse.

He moved swiftly to his sergeant's side. "They still there?"

As an answer a rifle spoke from among the trees, the bullet struck the side of the log wall, a glancing blow, and went screaming on in a ricochet.

One haystack flamed high, lighting the whole yard. The other had not yet thoroughly caught and was producing more smoke than flame.

Reese took time to assess their position. They were in no real danger from the hidden attackers so long as they held their places, but they were pinned down. There was no chance of Blunt, Ellis, or himself crossing the yard to where most of the horses had bunched behind the hay barn, caught there in the el of the building against the poles of the corral fence.

But he could see Bo and Gil Martin in the barn's shadow and he cupped his hands, calling across to them in Gulf French.

The brothers were Cajun, small dark men, fearless and very dangerous with either gun or knife.

"Catch your horses, ride back, keep the barn between you and the brush as long as you can then slant off and get in the timber. Dig these bastards out for me. We'll cover you."

He heard their ready response and turned, saying to Blunt, "As soon as they're mounted pour it in."

He had dropped his own rifle to go after the girl, and now snatched it from the ground and ran along the house front, crouching down at Whitey Ellis' side.

"Give them hell when the Martins ride."

Whitey showed him a tight-lipped smile. Three years younger than Reese, he had been raised at the old Triple X and in some ways was closer to Reese than his brother Alf had ever been.

They waited, watching the Cajuns find their horses and lift themselves into the saddles. As they swung away he raised his rifle and drove a shot into the wall of trees.

At once Blunt and Ellis were firing, steadily, mechanically, and from the cook shack Pop Greer and Austin added their guns to the fusillade.

They worked methodically. With no one visible to shoot at and too much light now from the burning stacks for them to see the flash of the attackers' guns, they sent their bullets into the area, forcing the unseen men to shelter themselves for their own protection.

The Martins left the haven of the hay shed and drove their horses hard, out of range, down the lane toward the distant gate. Short of the road they slowed and split, one riding north, one south across the uneven valley floor, and circled the ranch buildings in a huge arc.

Carstairs maintained the covering barrage until the roll of the land hid them from view, then he breathed a sigh of relief and signaled his cease-fire.

He had little fear for the Martins. They

were like Indians. They could creep through brush without disturbing a twig and they had handled knives since early childhood, without sound, with the deadliness of a striking bushmaster.

There was a time of silence, of tense listening in the red, dancing light of the yard. An occasional shot rang from the brush as if the men concealed there wanted to remind them of their presence. There was no way to tell the progress of the grim hunt going on in the heavy gloom of the timber.

It seemed years before a sudden burst of yells and gunfire brought the fight to life, but no bullets struck the ranch buildings. Then there was silence again before Bo Martin's voice reached across the yard.

"They pulled out."

He stepped into shadowy view, leading his horse, followed a minute later by his brother. They mounted and rode in to Carstairs, tight, mirthless smiles on their dark faces.

"We got two of them, and hit a horse as they took off."

"How many were there?"

"Four went clean. I don't think they'll be back for a while." Bo patted the knife swinging in its sheath at his hip.

Carstairs said, "Good. Get the horses unsaddled, then see what you can do about the stacks." He turned away, crossing the yard to kneel for a moment beside the fallen Taylor, to touch the still brow with his warm hand.

Bitter grief rose in him. The boy had survived the rigors of the Mexican campaign to die here in this yard that should have meant safety for him. At least Taylor had had one look at the lush land where he would rest.

Whitey Ellis came to stand beside him wordlessly.

Carstairs said, "Take him in the bunkhouse. We'll bury him in the morning."

Ellis nodded, keeping his eyes on Taylor.

"How's Nell?"

"She twisted her knee when she fell. I'll check."

He rose tiredly as the cook came up behind them to say, "How about some chow and coffee?"

Carstairs nodded. "Thanks. We haven't had a decent meal for weeks."

"Make it years." Whitey Ellis looked up, grinning his crooked, small-boy grin.

Carstairs left them, going to the house. He found the girl in a rear bedroom beside a crib, trying to quiet the baby in her arms.

A boy of two watched him with large dark eyes so like his mother's that Reese found them startling. The boy made no sound, showed no fear, and Reese bent above the bed to speak reassuringly and put out one hand to pat the soft cheek.

Behind him the baby's crying stopped. Nell laid it gently in the crib and straightened as

Carstairs turned. Her face was very white, and her mouth worked a little.

"Have they gone?"

He nodded. Unconsciously he opened his arms and as unconsciously she came into them, burying her head against his shoulder, trembling.

"Oh, Reese, Reese, if anything had happened to them."

"Nothing did." His voice was not quite steady, but it was more her nearness than his worry over the children that shook him.

He bent his head and kissed the softness of her hair, then cupped a hand under her chin and raised her mouth to his. She tried to draw away but he was too strong for her.

A voice behind them said harshly, "Turn around."

Reese let her go slowly. He turned. His brother Alf stood spread-legged in the doorway, a gun in his hand.

THREE

It was the girl who moved, the girl who was between them as her husband brought up the heavy gun.

"No, Alf. Wait. It's Reese."

For a moment there was no comprehension in Alf Carstairs' handsome face. He stared at the man standing behind his wife. Then he let the gun hand fall until the weapon pointed at the floor, and passed a hand uncertainly across his eyes.

"Reese? Reese is dead."

"Not quite," said Reese, and grinned.

Alf continued to stare. "In the name of God, where did you drop from?"

"Mexico, and it was a long, hot way."

Nell's voice cut in. "I met him and his men in town. When we got here Creed was attacking the ranch. He'd have burned the house."

"The Raiders? Is that who's outside?"

"Didn't you recognize them? Whitey's with me, and Joe Blunt, the Martin brothers, Pop Greer, Austin. Taylor rode up with us. He got his from Creed's men here."

"Wait." Alf spun around. They heard him run down the hall and heard his hoarse voice as he shouted across the yard.

The girl turned slowly. Her eyes were level, her tone steady.

"There's something you have to know, Reese, something you must understand. I don't love you, I love Alf. It will be better for us all if you accept that fact now."

"It isn't the truth." His voice was suddenly wild with protest. "You're saying so because you don't want trouble between us."

"No."

The baby started to cry again and she turned away. "Please go on out. Please leave me alone."

He went automatically. Rising within him was a fierce anger against the fate that had dealt him this final crushing, ruining blow, that had in a matter of hours wiped out all the plans for the future which had nourished him through his wandering.

In the yard his brother was surrounded by men, talking excitedly.

"We made a mistake. We didn't know you. We saw you around the stacks and thought it was Creed."

Reese counted quickly. "Anyone get hurt?"

"Fortunately, no. Duke Borden was in the lead and Blunt recognized him and called his name."

"Duke here?"

"He just went to tell Pete to feed the whole crew. He's my foreman."

"What happened to old Jake?"

"When I got back to Texas, he was too crippled up to make the drive. I hired Duke." Alf pushed through the crowd to shake hands with Whitey, with Joe Blunt. Then he raised his voice to his own riders. "You boys introduce yourselves and take care of these men. I rode with them all through the war. Bury Creed's men up on the hill. We'll try to get the circuit rider out for Taylor tomorrow."

He came back to Reese's side as the crews scattered, and there was strain in his manner which had not been there before.

"Reese, I really thought you were dead."

"Where'd you get that idea?" The red glow from the burning stacks showed him his brother's face plainly.

"Sam Holland brought the news out of Mexico four years ago. He said you'd been executed by a firing squad."

Reese felt his stomach turn with nausea. Sam Holland had not come out of Mexico four years ago. Sam Holland had never come out of Mexico. He had occupied the bunk next to Reese in the hut at the prison ranch through the full years of their captivity. He had started north with them when they escaped, but he had stopped a sniper's bullet during one of their running engagements with Juarez's men.

"Sam told you that?"

"He didn't tell me. I wasn't in Texas when he crossed the border, but Duke was. Duke wrote me the word."

Reese considered this carefully. Who was lying, Alf or Duke? Alf had robbed him of Nell and might be trying to claim the whole ranch. What could Borden hope to gain by a report that Reese was dead?

And then an answer came, ready-made, to his mind. Duke Borden was a climber. Reese knew it now in this moment of sharp clarity. Duke Borden had always been a climber.

The family had amounted to very little in the days before the war. Reese's father had frowned from the first on Reese's desire to marry Nell, and his stepmother had refused to have the Bordens in the house, had always tried to keep the two apart.

All through the courtship Duke Borden had helped, carrying notes between them, taking his sister to dances where he knew Reese would be, putting himself out in every way to help the younger man, even enlisting when Reese and three others had first formed the Raiders.

Counting him as a friend it was doubly difficult to understand his motive in this lie unless even the friendship had had a motive. But if Duke had decided that Reese would never come out of Mexico, if he had wanted his sister married to the Triple X, then it would have to be Alf, not Reese she married.

He saw Duke Borden leave the cook shack and stride toward them. There was no mistaking the huge man. He stood six feet four, a broad, dark-haired man with a heavy face and the most powerful hands Reese had ever seen.

He came up now, the grin on his big face, his hand hard in Reese's grasp but his black eyes watchful, studying Reese as if trying to decide whether the younger man knew of his treachery.

Nothing in Reese's lined face told of suspicion and his voice was warm as he said, "Like old times, Duke."

Borden nodded jovially. "It is that, Captain. It is that. Like having the Raiders riding all over again. The cook's got grub on the table. Come and eat."

Alf interrupted him. "Have Pete serve the men and then bring plates for us to the house. I want a chance to talk to Reese alone."

Borden glanced at him, opened his mouth as though to protest, then closed it slowly. "See you later, Captain."

"And find someplace for the others to sleep. Reese will use the spare room."

"I'll stay with them," Reese said. "I couldn't sleep in a bed, it's been too long since I saw one."

They watched Borden go, then Alf took his

arm and ushered him toward the house. In the hall Alf said, "You'll want to wash up. The bench is on the back porch. I'll check on Nell and the children." He stepped into the children's bedroom and closed the door.

Reese stood looking at the door with a feeling of being completely shut out. Once he had shared the lives of these two people. Now he was almost a stranger in this house which he himself had ordered built.

He went on, and found the rear gallery. The burning stacks still lighted the yard with their crimson glow. The men had given up hope of saving either, since they were so far from the creek, and the smell of burning hay lay like a heavy mantle over the ranch.

He lifted down the tin pan from its nail on the wall above the bench, and went into the kitchen. The fire in the range burned low but the water in the reservoir was still hot. With the aid of the dipper he filled the pan and returned to the porch. It was luxury to have hot water and he soaped his hands and face and arms well, rinsing them first with hot, then with cold water from the bucket at the end of the bench.

Afterward he picked up the comb and tried to bring order to the long, tangled hair which fell nearly to his collar line. The face which stared back at him from the mirror was one he barely recognized. He did not wonder that his brother had failed to know him.

The hair was gray, nearly white, the beard grizzled with gray and the face beneath it was lined from bad food and the hardships he had endured. It could have been the face of a man of sixty. Instead, he had barely passed his thirtieth birthday.

Refreshed, his wet hair parted and slicked back, he went again into the house and along the hall to the front parlor. Alf was there before him, an embarrassed Alf who said,

"Nell has a headache from all the excitement. She's gone to bed."

Reese nodded and sank wearily into a split-backed rawhide chair. There was a bottle of whiskey on the table, with two glasses.

"Drink?"

"A very light one. It's been a long time and I'm beat."

He sat watching as his brother poured the liquor, wondering if Alf had really believed the story Duke had told of meeting Sam Holland or if the two of them had cooked it up to make the girl forsake her promise to wait.

Alf handed the glass across. "How'd you get away?"

"Another revolution down there now. Juarez is going to win, I think, but Diez's men captured the ranch where we were prisoners and offered to free us if we joined him. We did. There were only eighteen of us left by then. We fought three skirmishes with government troops and got whipped in all of them, so those of us who were still alive had a powwow and decided to head for the border. That was nearly five months ago. We lost ten men before we crossed the river, but some of us made it."

"What happened to the emperor?"

Reese Carstairs shrugged. The whiskey lay in a hot ball at the pit of his empty stomach, making him lightheaded. It didn't matter, really. The emperor had been in his grave a long time, dead, dead as the lost cause.

"You probably know most of it. After you and the boys pulled out in October the emperor fled to Orizaba. He was going to abdicate."

"I know that." Alf paced restlessly back and forth before his brother's chair. "If you'd only listened to me. If you'd only come with me."

Reese shrugged again. "I couldn't. I'd promised him I'd stay, but I wish I'd sent the full troop with you. Have any trouble getting out?"

It was Alf's turn to shrug. "Not as much as you might think. When you've got nearly fifty men at your back people tend to get out of your way. We had one real fight before we made Veracruz, but once there we sold our horses and got a ship for New Orleans. I was in the States thirty days after I left you.

"So he didn't abdicate."

"The French talked him out of it, damn

them. If he'd quit then Juarez had promised him a safe passage to Europe. The empress was already over there, trying to get further help.

"Instead he went back to Mexico City and took personal command of the army. He dragged us along as a guard of honor, and for a while it looked as if we might win, but in March instead of sending more help, Napoleon suddenly pulled out what French troops we had.

"I tried again to get Maximilian to run, but he wouldn't. When our native forces deserted to the revolutionaries he surrendered."

Reese broke off, visualizing the scene in his mind, the proud Austrian, descendant of a hundred kings, standing before the firing squad.

"They court-martialed and shot him in June. At the last we were about the only men he had. They put us in prison in Veracruz. Why we weren't shot we couldn't figure until one of Juarez's generals showed up and offered to save us if we would work for him.

"We soon found out what he meant. We were no better than slaves on his ranch. He had a man with a gun watching us every minute. How any of us survived I'll never know."

"Wonder what made Holland think you were dead?"

Reese said carefully, "I wouldn't know."

"When did you see him last?"

"I'm hardly sure of that either." He was not ready to bring the lie into the open, not yet.

Alf rubbed a hand across his eyes and his tone turned uneasy.

"About Nell. She waited a long time."

"I know." Reese felt that his face was suddenly frozen, the skin across his jaws too tight to allow proper speech.

"I don't suppose you know that when we were kids I loved her too?"

"I didn't."

"Well, I used to be jealous as hell of you. I think that was the main reason you and I were never very close."

Reese could have added that Alf's mother had done everything in her power to prevent their being close. She had never forgiven Reese that he and not his father was the actual owner of the Triple X, that his mother in dying had willed the ranch to him instead of to her husband.

Alf's mother had not known this at the time of her marriage, and she had been selfish and grasping. As Reese remembered her she was a gaunt-faced, penny-pinching person.

"Now we're married." Alf was still having difficulty in talking. "She told me a little while ago that she loves me."

"She told me so too." Suddenly, much to

his surprise, Reese felt sorry for his brother. He realized that if Alf had not been a party to the lie about his death, the man must be in almost as much mental torment as himself.

"Forget it. My coming home can't make any difference between us, and have you taken a good look at me? What woman wants a broken-down wreck who could be a hundred and ten?"

Alf brightened. He came over to take Reese's glass and refill it.

"Here's to all of us. We'll ride into Walden tomorrow and see the lawyer. We'll split the ranch just like we planned. Then we'll take care of Creed."

They drank silently.

The cook came in, carrying three steaming plates, followed by Duke Borden with three cups of coffee.

Alf swung around. The liquor had touched him and heightened the relief Reese's words had brought him.

"Have a drink, both of you, to the Triple X, to the Carstairs brothers. Ben Creed's not got one man to fight. He's got two. He's as good as finished right now."

FOUR

Reese had not slept enough. Dawn was pink above the mountains before he had dragged himself into the hay barn where Joe Blunt had arranged his blankets. The whiskey plus his overwhelming fatigue and the heady surety that he had at last come home had drugged him.

He had been too tired to think even of Nell and what her marriage would mean to him.

He roused to find Alf bending over him, one hand gently shaking his shoulder. Around him his Raiders still slept, Joe Blunt spread on his back, his mouth wide, his snores even, regular, and surprisingly soft.

Reese clawed awake, hearing horses in the yard, and blinked groggily at his brother. Alf was grinning.

"Time to ride if we want to make Walden by noon."

Reese kicked back the blankets. He was fully dressed save for his patched boots. He stooped to pull them on, then followed Alf to the shed door, squinting against the sharp, bright light of the morning sun. Behind him his men had not stirred.

Alf led him to the cook shack and they sat facing across the scarred table, the warmth of their feeling for each other welling like the steam from the coffee in the big crockery cups.

Memory was heavy on them, and unguarded in their eyes; memory of another cookhouse a thousand miles to the south, of the old crew, of their father sitting cold and austere at the head of his table, of their father riding out to war, leaving Reese in charge of the ranch, and of the day when they had decided that they too must put on the uniform.

They had breakfasted together that morning also. Together they had ridden away, neither dreaming that it would be long years before they would sit thus at their own table again.

They talked little and ate rapidly, Alf being in haste to start for town, but there was between them a comfortable bond, an augur of good for their combined future.

There was no sign of Nell or the two children when they came from the cook shack and crossed to the horses tethered at the corral fence, but Duke Borden stood in the door of the blacksmith shop watching as they swung into the saddles.

Borden raised a hand and Reese returned the salute before he pulled his horse around and followed Alf along the lane toward the distant road.

They saw no one. The morning was theirs in the meadow, the land lush around them, cattle grazing in small bunches, cattle lying in the shade of the green trees bordering the shining creeks, fat cattle, their coats glistening.

Alf indicated the valley with a sweep of his arm.

"Probably the best range in North America."

He pointed to a hill rising from the level grass on their right. "I suggest you build your house there."

Reese looked at him quickly. It had not occurred to him that he would stay anywhere except at the present place.

Alf saw the look and color come up under the leather brownness of his skin, and he said in an apologetic voice, "It isn't that Nell and I don't want you in the house, but with the two kids growing up there just isn't enough room."

Reese nodded and measured the hill more carefully, noting its three crowning trees. In some ways it was a better location than that of the main ranch.

They rode on, Alf expounding on the virtues of this land which he had found and built against his brother's homecoming, Reese appreciating everything, his eyes hungry on the luxuriance after the starvation of the parched countries he had known so long.

The trail wound up a draw almost against the western bench, into the timber that ran down the mountainside and cast a welcome shade, sheltering them from the increasing heat of the sun.

They had covered perhaps a mile up this draw when the first shot came. There was no warning. Alf, riding slightly in the lead, threw out his arms and pitched sideways from the saddle, and his horse spooked away.

Reese had been buried in his own thoughts at the moment. He jerked erect and a second bullet whined by his ear. Instinctively he crouched over the back of his horse, digging his spurs into the startled animal, driving ahead.

The crouch saved his life, for a third bullet grooved along his back, tearing his shirt and slicing his skin.

The horse was in full run when the next shot struck its neck. It stumbled, recovered itself, then stumbled again and went over in a complete somersault that tossed Reese beyond it to land hard on the ground at the base of a pine tree.

The fall knocked most of the wind out of him, but the urge to survive forced him to his hands and knees and he scrambled around the tree into the protection of the trail-side brush and there got cautiously to his feet.

He was apparently out of sight of the hidden marksman, for no further shots came. His rifle was still in the boot on his dead horse, and he did not relish running into the open to secure it.

But his brother was out there. He watched him and saw him stir and moved quickly back along the edge of the trail, using the rocks and timber as a shield, walking with stealthy care until he reached a point directly opposite Alf.

He saw his brother move again and called softly across the eight feet which now separated them.

"How bad you hit?"

There was no real answer, only a grumbled moan that slobbered off into silence. Reese stood for a long moment, steadying his breathing, measuring the distance and studying the footing. Then he plunged forward with the desperation of a man leaping into an ice-filled stream.

His rush apparently caught the sniper by surprise, for he had reached Alf's side, stooped and gathered up the larger man as he might a baby, and was turning when the rifle cracked again.

The bullet struck Alf. He could feel it jar through his brother's body.

Another shot nicked his own shoulder close to the base of his neck, and then he was struggling into the timber, hearing the continuing spat of the rifle somewhere above him, the whanging impact of the bullets as they searched between the trees.

Had he not been handicapped with Alf he would have tried to locate the attacker, but his one thought now was to find a safe spot for the wounded man.

He found it where a burst of huge rocks reached out of the brush. Water had scooped a depression at the base of the rocks large enough for them both to lie in, and he bent over his brother, stripping away the shirt to stare in giddying hopelessness at the two purplish holes torn through the white body. One was high and had broken ribs and passed through the lungs. The other had caught Alf in the stomach, and gone out at his side.

Reese Carstairs had seen more than his share of bullet wounds, and he knew that Alf had no chance to survive, but even as he concluded that his brother was already dead the younger man's eyes flickered open and gazed up with consciousness and understanding.

"How bad?" It was a whisper.

Reese made no attempt to lie. They had been raised in a hard school and death had ridden as a familiar at their shoulders.

"Bad."

The eyes closed as if Alf had used up all

of his strength, then they opened again, the man's iron will forcing his broken body to respond.

"Take care of the kids." His voice was a shadow. "See that Nell is all right, and don't hold it against her that she married me. She needs you, Reese. This is no country for a woman to face alone."

The eyes closed again, his hand came out, groping, and Reese gripped it with his own, feeling the sudden relaxation as his brother expired.

He squatted there, wondering at the pattern which fate wove. By all the laws of chance it should be he who was dead, not Alf. Alf had gotten out of Mexico while Reese remained through war and prison and torture, yet somehow he had managed to stay alive.

He might as well have been riding in the lead this morning instead of trailing a horse's length behind, in which case the sniper would have hit him first.

He knew a sudden burning, all consuming hatred of this unknown man who had sat safely above and deliberately cut off a human life.

Reese Carstairs did not know how many men he himself had killed, but these had been killed in the heat of battle, and always he had been risking his life against theirs. But he meant to kill a man coldly now.

He loosened his holstered gun and checked

it, then as quietly as a shadow he left the depression and worked upward through the brush, circling to the right, hoping to come upon the bushwhacker from above.

But he had hardly started to climb when he heard the quick rush of the horse and knew that his man was riding out. He stopped, trying to peer through the trees for at least a glimpse of the fleeing figure, but the pole pine grew so close together that it was like looking at a stockade wall.

The noise of the retreating horse died. Reese stood yet awhile, listening, motionless, then he dropped down to the trail, collecting his rifle before he started the walk back to the ranch.

He judged that they had come about five miles, and it was the longest five miles he had ever traveled. His feet in his broken boots blistered, the sun was hot to the point of near danger and the flies found his shoulder wound. But nothing drove his grief from his mind, nor the knowledge that he must be the one to bring the news of her husband's death to Nell.

All during the grim hike Reese puzzled over the identity of the attacker, wondering whether the assault had been directed at Alf, at himself, or at both of them. Certainly the man, whoever he was, had tried hard to kill Reese as well as his brother.

Emotionally and physically spent, he turned

into the lane and limped toward the ranch house.

Joe Blunt squatted in the shade of the hay barn when Reese came into the lower yard. Two men were building a box behind the blacksmith shop and Duke Borden stood at the corral fence watching his riders break out a string of new horses.

Duke turned to stare at Reese, then Blunt lurched up and began to run forward. Duke Borden's long strides brought him swiftly across the hard-baked ground, and the three met just beside the cook shack.

"What the hell happened?"

Reese told them tensely and watched Borden's face freeze into rocky, sculptured lines. Without a word the foreman swung toward the house. Joe Blunt hurried back to the hay barn.

Reese hesitated for an instant, then followed Borden to where he stopped at the steps, calling, "Nell, Nell," and they saw Nell Carstairs appear in the open doorway.

"What is it?"

Duke's voice was ugly with strain. "Alf's dead."

She stood unmoving, her face without expression as if her mind failed to grasp the meaning of his words. Then the whisper came, for it was little more than a whisper.

"Dead? How?"

"Bushwhacked."

"Who?" It was still a whisper.

"Creed. Who else?"

Slowly she came across the porch and stopped to lean against one of its posts. She was not crying, but her face was set in a mask of shock, her mind still refusing reality beyond a certain point.

Duke Borden pulled out a red handkerchief and wiped his head, his eyes suspiciously moist.

"Damn Creed for the murdering bastard he is. I'll hang him before I'm through. I'll hang him."

She looked toward Reese, for the first time aware that he was beside her brother.

"How did it happen?"

Reese told her briefly.

"And you weren't hit?"

Silently he turned so that she could see the gash on his neck, the streak burned across his back beneath the bloody shirt.

Duke was already gone, shouting orders at the men in the corral. Joe Blunt and Whitey Ellis came from the hay barn, the rest of the Raiders tumbling after them at a half-run. Nell watched unseeing, then without speaking again, went into the house.

Reese's men gathered silently around him and they walked slowly toward the corral where Duke was telling the story to his riders.

Two caught up their horses quickly, mounted, and leading a third horse, drove out of the yard.

Joe Blunt was at Reese's elbow. He said in an undertone, "Who were they? How many?"

Reese shook his head. "Borden seems to think it was Creed."

"And you don't?"

Reese shrugged. He did not want to say it aloud, but he could not forget that Duke had lied about his own death. He knew that he would never again trust Duke Borden.

A group of riders came into the yard from the north and Borden swung around, shouting to them.

"Alf's been shot."

They ran their horses across to him and he waved them off, bawling, "Creed bush-whacked him on the bench. Get into town, get the sheriff, and if that circuit-riding preacher's there, bring him on out."

Without stopping they swerved down the lane. Motion in the yard ceased with their leaving.

The remainder of Alf's crew rode in one by one. There were a good dozen around the corral when the men who had gone for Alf's body returned. There was no talking. Silence held them all.

The three horses came up the lane with the blanket-wrapped burden strapped across the lead animal, and Nell appeared again on the porch.

She stood at the top of the steps. There were still no tears. In silence she waited until they had ridden almost to the porch rail, trailed by the men on foot before she said, "Bring him into the house."

There was no inflection in her tone. Without glancing at any of them she turned back to the door. As she reached it she swayed and put out one hand gropingly as if suddenly blind, caught the jamb, steadied herself and went on inside.

The riders swung out of their saddles, the crew crowding around, loosening the ropes, lifting Alf's body down, carrying him up the steps and into the coolness of the house. Reese followed.

Nell Carstairs quietly indicated the bed in the rear room and they laid him there and left. She did not look up as Reese and Duke remained. She gave no sign that she was conscious of their presence.

Her brother crossed to her and awkwardly put a hand on her shoulder. Still she did not stir.

Reese looked at them and again felt himself excluded, shut out, unwanted. He backed away and returned to the yard where small clusters of men talked together in low tones, where Borden's two riders were unsaddling at the corral. He felt completely alone.

He walked to the hay barn and drew Whitey Ellis aside. The bond between these two was strong. Ellis had never really liked Alf, for the younger Carstairs had been inclined to bully him in their childhood, but he said gravely now, "Maybe we should go looking for this Creed."

Reese shrugged. He had not voiced any suspicion yet, but he trusted both Ellis' loyalty and his judgment.

"I'm not sure it was Creed who killed him."

Whitey's drawn face with its tangle of grayed beard came around quickly.

"Meaning?"

"Meaning that Duke lied about meeting Sam Holland. He said Holland told him I was dead. We both know that Holland never came out of Mexico. He lied, I think, to stop his sister from waiting for me, to make her marry Alf."

"Why?"

Reese sighed deeply. "I guess for the same reason he tried to marry her to me when we were kids, so he'd have some connection with the Triple X. I can't think of any other reason."

Whitey was watching him with sharp curiosity.

"You implying that you think Duke Borden murdered Alf?"

"Oh, he didn't pull the trigger himself, but when I gave Alf the bill of sale for the cattle from the old ranch the understanding was that he and I would share equally in the new place he would build."

"I know that."

"Last night Alf made plans for us to go in to the lawyer today and get the papers drawn up. Duke was in the hall when he said it. Maybe he didn't want me to share in the ranch. Maybe he wanted it all for his sister. The easiest way to keep it so would be to get rid of Alf."

"Or you."

Reese said, "Whoever killed him tried to get me too. What would happen if we both died? The ranch would go to Nell, of course, and Duke would run it for her."

Whitey was silent for a long time, then he nodded.

"What are you going to do?"

Reese blew out his breath strongly and straightened, wincing at the stab of pain from his bandaged shoulder.

"First, see if I can rustle up some grub for us all. Then I'm going to borrow some scissors and a razor. I'm going to cut your hair and let you cut mine. I'm tired of looking like a wild man."

He motioned to his men, still standing apart in a quiet group, and started toward the cook shack.

It was nearly evening before the sheriff rode in, bringing five men and the circuit rider. They buried Alf Carstairs and Taylor above the creek on a small knoll which looked out across the rolling grass.

There were few words as the long line followed the crude boxes up the winding path. Nell walked behind with Duke Borden at her side, she carrying the baby, her brother carrying the older child, at the head of the Triple X crew.

Reese's six remaining riders came next, leaving Reese to bring up the rear, sensing that he wanted to be alone at this time.

He was still in the yard when the horse swung from the main road and raced up the curving lane. Reese turned as it reached the corral and realized that the rider was a girl and thought it must be a neighbor, perhaps a friend of Nell's.

He had borrowed a shirt from one of the regular crew. His white hair was trimmed and enhanced rather than detracted from his deep blue eyes. His beard was gone, and despite the lines which the years and trouble had etched on his face he looked far younger than when he had ridden in on the preceding night, yet he noted with a wry pang the grace and youth of the girl as she stepped lightly from the saddle and ran up the path toward him, feeling that his own youth was eaten away.

She stopped in front of him a little breathless, looking up expectantly.

"Reese," she said, "Reese, don't you remember me? I'm Jenny."

She was a small girl, dark, with black eyes and a quick, mobile face that came to full life when she smiled, and she was smiling now. He stared at her. He knew her, but in the time he had been away she had grown from a child with pigtails into a woman. He counted back, trying to guess her age, and decided that she must be near twenty.

"You don't look quite the same."

He saw now that she had Nell's eyes, yet deeper, blacker.

"You never even looked at me in those days."

There was a light note in her voice but the smile was gone from her red lips.

"I used to follow you around at a distance whenever you came over to see Nell. And when you joined the Raiders and rode back in uniform, remember? I cried and you kissed me good-by."

He had forgotten that. There had been only an hour and he had wanted it alone with Nell. Instead, the whole family had crowded around him, four children younger than Nell, two boys and two girls. He had paid little attention to any of them just then. He did remember that one of the girls had cried, that she had flung herself into his arms in near hysteria, this little Jenny who had been a sort of mascot to him.

"I remember." He brought up a smile from somewhere within him.

They were moving slowly up the hill after the funeral party. Her voice changed.

"What happened to Alf? I heard in town that he was dead."

His tone was careful, studied. "He was shot this morning."

"By whom?"

"It might have been Creed."

"Creed?"

"That's what they tell me."

Her face turned thoughtful, almost bleak. "Ben Creed's a hard man. He and Alf have fought bitterly about the north range but I don't think he'd bushwhack anyone."

"You know him personally?"

"He wants me to marry him."

Reese Carstairs was startled. "Marry you? Marry the sister-in-law of the man he was fighting?"

She said tonelessly, "The Triple X and I have not been the best of friends."

She broke off as the group ahead stopped, and they caught up with the Raiders. The men split to give her passage and she went on to her sister's side, silently taking the baby in her arms, standing quiet between Nell and Duke through the long, droning service.

Reese made no attempt to go with her. He remained with Whitey Ellis and the others, the seven of them, hardly conscious of the circuit rider's words. Afterward he led the procession down the hill to the yard below.

He rounded the corner of the corral and

heard someone behind him and turned to find the sheriff at his elbow.

"Talk to you for a minute?"

The sheriff's name was Hawthorne, a slight man with yellow-gray hair and drooping mustache and an ineffectual air. It was only when you looked in his eyes that you realized he was someone out of the ordinary. They were blue and hard and cold as chipped ice.

Reese nodded.

"I understand you just rode in last night."

Again Reese nodded.

"Been in Mexico a long time, the way I hear it."

"Since the war."

"Never surrendered, huh?"

"No."

"Don't imagine anyone much cares. I was on the other side."

Reese looked at him levelly. Once this statement would have struck at his emotion. It no longer did. All the bitterness and humiliation of defeat were gone, driven out of him.

"Thanks. I'd better hunt up someone to surrender to."

"Haven't an idea who it would be. Also hear you used to court your brother's wife, that she only married him when she thought you were dead."

Reese's eyebrows arched up. "You seem to know a lot about me."

"From her sister. Jenny's a pal of mine.

Heard her talk about you a lot of times. Fine girl, Jenny. More than I can say for the rest of the family. Oh, I don't mean Nell Carstairs or Duke. They're all right from what I can find out, but the old man and the two younger boys and the other sister are trash."

Reese said nothing.

"Think Creed killed your brother?"

"I don't know who it was. Whoever did it fired from the brush and I didn't see him."

"That's what Mart January told me when I rode in. What do you think of Mart?"

"I haven't exchanged a dozen words with him."

The sheriff pulled a worn pipe from his coat pocket and filled it deliberately.

"Where were you riding when Alf was shot, ahead or behind him?"

"Behind him."

"Horse got shot in the side of the neck. I stopped to take a look."

Reese Carstairs' thin lips quirked slightly. There was no humor in the gesture. "Are you suggesting that maybe I shot Alf because of his wife?"

"You didn't, did you?"

"Would you believe me if I said no?"

Hawthorne took time to light his pipe, to draw on it deeply, to let the smoke curl out from below the ragged edge of his long mustache.

"I think so. Yes, I'm sure of it." He nodded

sharply and marched away.

Reese watched him go, so intent that he did not see Duke Borden come from the house, did not know that Borden was heading toward him until the big man spoke.

"Nell wants you."

"Where is she?"

"In the house." Borden did not linger but moved on around the corral after the sheriff.

Reese went immediately to the house, knocked on the partly open door and heard Nell's voice tell him to come in. He found her sitting on the sofa where he had placed her after her fall from the buckboard, and saw that Jenny was with her.

He stopped just inside the door, a sudden welling of tenderness for her damming his words, and her voice cut cold across the moment.

"I hate to say this, Reese, but the way things are and the way it has been between us I think it would be better if you didn't stay at the ranch."

His head jerked back visibly, as if he had been dealt a blow.

"Not stay at the ranch? But who's going to run it?"

"Duke, of course."

Reese Carstairs took a long, slow breath, controlling himself with effort.

"But Nell, you know that the Triple X is mine, that I signed the cattle over to Alf only to simplify it for him in establishing this place. The understanding was that he and I would be partners. Last night he said we'd go in and have the papers drawn up today. We were on our way when he was shot."

A stony hardness masked her face, such as he had never seen there before.

"Reese, I can't believe that Alf would so lightly hand over half of everything he worked so hard to build. Even if he would, I don't feel at liberty to do so. The ranch really belongs to the children. I can't give away half their birthright."

Somehow he got out of the room, out of the house. He was staggered, hit in the stomach with a gun butt. Bad enough that it should happen, but to have Nell do this to him was incomprehensible. Bitterness flowed through him, bitterness to eat away his reason.

FIVE

They were within two miles of Walden, and they had ridden most of the distance from the ranch in stunned silence. Behind them, keeping well back so as not to intrude, rode the six men, all that were left of the Raiders. They too were silent, turned sullen and weary again after the brief view of hope.

Whitey Ellis had been especially angry. Only Carstairs' absolute order had prevented him from storming into the house and confronting Nell.

Jenny Borden broke the silence. "There's no call to be standoffish, Reese. You and your men must stay somewhere. I run a hotel. I have empty rooms."

"We're broke." Reese faced rigidly ahead toward the lights of the clustered town. "Not only broke, we have no clothes other than what we're wearing, nothing but the guns we carry and the horses we ride. After last night's fracas we're nearly out of ammunition."

"I'd say the Bordens owe you something."

It was the first time she had mentioned the conversation in the ranch house. "That was a cruel thing she did, Reese, but very like her."

He looked at her profile, dim beneath the star-bright sky. She had little resemblance to Nell, though in her own way she was most attractive and there was a warm directness about her. But he did not understand her words.

"What do you mean by that? She's had a shock. She wasn't thinking straight."

Jenny Borden turned to face him squarely, unable to withhold her outburst.

"You're still in love with her, even after tonight, and when she finds that she needs you she'll call you back and you'll go."

He was still sick with the hurt of Nell Carstairs' words but he fought against the doubt her sister raised.

He nodded stiffly. "If she needs me . . ."

The girl spun around angrily. "That's the trouble with you and I've always known it. Let anyone say they need you and you're Johnny-on-the-spot. You're stronger than most and you feel bound to use that strength in blind devotion.

"Why did you stay in Mexico when Alf and Duke and the others rode north? Wasn't it to help the emperor when everyone else had deserted him?"

He found no answer. He was bewildered by her vehemence.

"And you never surrendered. You couldn't even forsake a cause that was totally lost. And you're still loyal to Nell. You leap to her defense when I tell you she'll use you again. But listen to me, Reese. There's no loyalty in her."

He shook his head. "I don't understand you. Certainly she waited until she thought I was dead before she married Alf, for instance."

Jenny Borden scoffed. "Who was there in Texas to marry during the war? No one but old men and boys. She set her cap for Alf as soon as he came back to Texas. It was Alf who would not marry her until he believed you were never coming home."

He stared at her. "You're saying she was a party to the lie Duke told about meeting Sam Holland?"

"What lie?"

"Holland never came out of Mexico. I buried him myself."

She made a little moaning sound and then was silent.

"Aren't you going to answer my question?"

Her voice was suddenly tired. "What's the use. What is done is done. But I actually don't think she knew. She had already decided to marry a small rancher over on the Sabine River. Duke didn't want that. Alf was in love with her and Duke told him you were dead. Duke pushed the marriage to work himself into the ranch. We all watched it."

"Is that why you haven't married, because of the shortage of men?"

"Partly."

"What other reasons?"

"We aren't talking about me," she said, and touched her spurs to her horse and drove into town.

The Raiders moved up around him, lending him the strength of their old group unity, but Reese was alone, thinking, and his faith in Nell Carstairs flicked out and died.

Jenny was waiting for them when they came up to the hotel.

"You're staying here." It was a flat statement, not a question. "The barn's around back. Take my horse along and rub him down, will you?"

She handed him the reins as if never questioning his agreement, and hurried into the building.

Reese swung his horse to look at his men. For himself he would have refused, but the sheer exhaustion he read in the drooping figures was too much for him. All during the hard trek north they had buoyed up their flagging strength with dreams of what they would do when they reached the ranch.

"Come on."

He led them along the dust track beside the hotel building and into the yard before the barn.

Joe Blunt found a lantern dangling from a nail in the wide door frame and lighted it. By its yellow glow they unsaddled, wordlessly rubbed down the horses, and turned them into the grass corral. Then, carrying their blankets as if they were rolls of sheet lead, they slogged single file into the hotel.

Reese came into the kitchen first, the men close at his heels, to find Jenny at the big range, her face already flushed with the heat. It made her even more attractive. She turned and smiled at them.

"The wash bench is out back. Supper in ten minutes."

The men dropped their blankets in a corner and dragged out, leaving Reese alone with the girl.

"You don't have to feed us."

She was matter-of-fact. "Stop the heroics, Captain. You have to eat."

He said, meaning it, "You're quite a person."

She considered him, her dark eyes unreadable. "Don't be grateful." Her tone strengthened with feeling. "The one thing I can't stand from you is gratitude. Now go and wash up."

He washed. They ate. Mush sliced and fried in sweet grease, a pile of steaks which vanished magically, and a deep-dish apple pie, the first Reese had tasted in nearly ten years.

The girl ate with them, sitting at the end of the long table in the narrow, barrack-like dining room. There was no conversation. The girl was indrawn, the men too tired to even try at politeness.

Afterward Reese and Whitey Ellis did the dishes while Jenny put fresh sheets on the beds.

Reese wakened with the sense that he had slept for a long time. Sunlight showed him the hotel room around him, a typical hotel room of the country, its wide board floor covered with braided rag rugs, its washstand marred by the carelessness of a hundred passing guests.

In the bed at his side Whitey Ellis still slept, his haggard face looking curiously childlike in repose.

He rose, trying not to stir the cornhusk mattress more than necessary, and used the cold water in the bowl to sponge his naked body. He dressed without disturbing the other man and moved to the window for a glance at the sky.

He had no watch, but from the position of the sun he judged it well before noon. He crossed to the door, opened it, and slipped into the hall. Faint noises reached him from below, and he thought he heard a baby cry. He went quietly down the stairs.

The sounds were coming from the kitchen. He hesitated, then threaded through the dining room and lobby and pushed open the kitchen door.

Nell Carstairs sat on a chair beside the big serving table, facing away from him, with the baby on her knees. The boy played on the floor at her feet with a rolling pin and two pans for toys.

Jenny worked at the sink, her back also toward the door. Neither saw Reese as he paused in the entrance.

"I told you you couldn't trust Duke." Jenny's voice was sharp. "It's your own fault. You did a terrible thing last night. Now that it's backfired you come whining around like a whipped pup."

"I'm not thinking of myself." These were tears in Nell Carstairs' voice. "I'm thinking of the children. What will happen to them?"

"Maybe Duke will give you money every month like he promised."

"Fifty dollars. What can I do with fifty dollars?"

"You lived on a lot less for many years."

The little boy looked up, saw Reese and scrambled to his feet. He ran across the kitchen to wrap his small arms about Reese's leg. His action made his mother turn and her eyes widened.

"Reese."

He stooped, picked up the boy and came forward to set him on the table.

"What is it now?"

Jenny spoke from the sink. "Duke's got the ranch."

Reese turned to gape at his brother's widow. "Duke's got the ranch? How do you mean?"

Jenny said, "Show him the copy of the will."

Nell drew a folded paper from the pocket of her dress and held it toward him silently. He opened it and read in increasing disbelief:

I, Alf Carstairs, being of sound mind, do hereby declare that this is my last will and testament and supersedes all previous wills.

I hereby leave one half of the ranch known as the Triple X, situated in the valley known as North Park in the Territory of Colorado, to my son, Lin Reese; one half of said ranch to my brother-in-law, Duke Borden; the whole to be operated by Borden as he sees fit until the twenty-first birthday of my son, when he, Lin Reese, shall inherit his half.

I purposely do not leave this ranch to my wife because it is impossible for a woman to either hold or operate property in this country without a man's help.

I further direct that out of the earnings of the ranch Duke shall pay my wife, Nell, a monthly amount sufficient to maintain her comfort and to raise our children.

Should anyone attempt to set this will aside, I ask the courts that they be barred from ever sharing in the Triple X Ranch.

Alf Carstairs

Reese's hand trembled as he folded the paper and laid it on the table at her side, but there was no softening in his face.

"Duke ask you to leave the ranch?"

Nell spread her hands in a frantic gesture.

"No, but Reese, I was so frightened. The way he acted when he showed this to me . . . I almost think it was he who had Alf killed. And if he'd do that Lin isn't safe at the ranch." She looked at the boy, a quick tremor shaking her. "He must be crazy. Pete thinks so." She caught his puzzled look and explained, "Pete Mullins, the cook at the Triple X. He quit this morning and brought the children and me here."

Reese remembered the stocky Irishman and wondered if there were others of the crew who felt loyalty to Alf, who would not work for Duke.

"Does Pete know anything about Duke, and Alf's death, or just suspect? Would there be others in the crew who might help pin it on Duke?"

She shook her head. "Pete's sure of it now but has no proof. He said three of the men quit when they heard about the will but they didn't know anything, just wouldn't stay with Duke. Pete was very loyal to Alf. He's gone to ask Moose Kobbler for a job at the store until he can sign on somewhere else. He wants to be on hand." Her voice broke. "Reese, you've got to stop Duke."

"I'll stop him," said Reese. "Duke Borden is not going to take over my ranch."

"Yours and Lin's." Nell put the baby on the floor and stood up, coming a step toward him. "I've got to explain about yesterday . . . to make you understand."

"Understand what?"

"I was so afraid of gossip. When I knew you were alive I wanted to come to you but I couldn't desert Alf. And last night I must have been hysterical. I was afraid of what they'd say. I'm not afraid now."

He shook his head. "It's no good."

"You mean you won't help me? Help little Lin?"

He sighed deeply. "Of course I'll help. I promised Alf I would. But there's no more for you and me."

He picked up the will and walked tiredly out of the kitchen.

SIX

The courthouse was plain, built of cut lumber, one of the few structures in the town not made of chinked logs, its boards weathered silver soft. Courtroom and county offices occupied the ground floor, the sheriff's office and jail filled the basement beneath them.

The building perched on the crest of a hill which fell away sharply at the rear, putting the windows on the west of the basement well above ground.

Reese Carstairs left his horse untethered before the hitch rail, certain that the animal would stand, head down in the building's shade, grateful to be quiet. He followed the path around the side, descended the stone steps and pushed open the sheriff's door.

Inside it was cool and semi-dark, and Hawthorne sat in shirtsleeves at the roll-top desk in the corner, his head bent over his monthly report. He turned as Reese entered, his lined face relaxing.

"Carstairs. Come in."

Reese nodded, pausing to adjust his eyes from their sun squint, then crossed the small room and laid Nell's copy of Alf's will before the man.

Hawthorne read it hastily, frowning, then leaned back in his chair for a more careful rereading. He placed it on the surface before him with studied slowness and looked up.

"Why would Alf do a thing like this?"

Reese sat against a corner of the desk. "Knowing Alf, I think I understand." He kept his voice expressionless. "He wanted to protect Nell. He was very much in love with her and his children and he knew that this is a dangerous country. I suppose there are still Indians in the hills."

"There are."

"I think Alf figured to insure Duke's staying and caring for them by giving him a half of the ranch. Alf was a trusting man. It would not have occurred to him to doubt Duke Borden."

The sheriff raised his boots to the top of the partly open drawer, fishing his pipe from his shirt pocket.

"And you do?"

Carstairs nodded. He told Hawthorne of the lie about Sam Holland and the false report of his own death.

"When I came up here everything Duke had planned went out the window. He knew Alf and I were riding to the lawyer to set up our partnership. Although it wasn't mentioned, he undoubtedly realized that Alf would alter his will, make me rather than Duke trustee for his children. I believe he sent a man to wait along the trail. I think he meant we should both be killed. I'd be a danger to Duke alive and he knew it."

Hawthorne drew his pipe to life. "These are pretty serious charges."

"I know. But follow it further. If he did kill Alf, and tried to kill me, he might as easily decide to get rid of Alf's son as well. Nell brought the children into town this morning."

The sheriff whistled softly. "I knew Jenny didn't like him too well but . . . you've shown me no proof to back up what you're saying. Were any of his men away from the ranch when you started for town?"

Carstairs shook his head. "I can't say. I'm not familiar with his crew. I got there only the night before." He shoved his hat to the back of his gray head. "What are we going to do about it? Duke's known me a long while. He knows I will not take this quietly. He'll expect me to come gunning for him."

The sheriff sat forward quickly. "Don't do that. Give me a chance to look into it." He sighed, then added, "Besides, I've seen him shoot. He's fast with a gun. Do you feel up to riding out, showing me where this sniper shot from?"

Carstairs nodded.

They rode easily through the heat, surrounded by the perfume from the deep meadowland, Carstairs saving his horse, Hawthorne old enough to have lost the need for rush. He questioned Reese, drawing out of him the story of the harsh years in Mexico, reading the marks they had left on the younger man, visualizing the ordeal and commenting,

"I don't think I'd have come through it. Not now for sure."

At the spot where Alf was killed Reese sat looking at the ground, again shaken by the surge of hatred for the assassin.

Hawthorne turned his horse into the timber and Reese followed, and they worked across the face of the bench, searching for a path to let them ride upward. They were a hundred feet above the bench when the sound of horses rose to them and they stopped.

Down through the trail a few feet of the road was still visible and Duke Borden with Mart January and another man rode slowly past. Reese Carstairs drew a sharp breath, the quick anger putting a salt taste in his mouth. He sensed the sheriff watching him, and knew the man half expected him to draw and fire at the unsuspecting trio.

He turned to give Hawthorne a brief tight grin, then put his horse upward again.

Hawthorne grunted. "Know why I asked

you about Mexico?"

"Yes."

". . . the way you've lived. The things you've been through. I didn't know about you."

"You know now?"

"Can't never be sure, but I don't think you'd shoot a man in the back."

Carstairs considered. "Where Duke's concerned, don't take a bet on it."

"Don't do it."

Carstairs rode in silence, nursing his bitter thoughts and at length they came upon the sniper's nest. Reese kept his seat, unwilling to put his foot on the same ground.

Hawthorne got down stiffly, reading the sign. Half a dozen cigarette butts, their brown paper wrappings still binding the shreds of tobacco, told that the man had waited for a long period.

From his saddle Reese spoke, controlling his voice that would have trembled with the depth of his feeling.

"Duke tried to lay the murder on Ben Creed. I don't believe Creed did it. Creed could not have known that Alf and I were riding this way and the ambush was not a chance thing."

Hawthorne nodded, not looking up. "Let's try to backtrack him."

He climbed his horse and again they searched the timber, finding the stomped ground where the bushwhacker's animal had stood, tied to a tree. The trail led on, up the mountain, and for a mile they had no difficulty following it. Then it curved northward onto a clearing of outcropping rock and sun-hardened ground.

Reese dismounted, walking ahead, picking out the man's track with difficulty until he lost it entirely.

They rode to the far edge of the clearing, crisscrossing its length, then tried to cut the trail within the trees, on the soft coat of needle and leaf mold. They could not find it again.

Hawthorne finally called a halt. "I thought I was a fair to middlin' tracker, but this boy really took some trouble to see he wasn't followed. We'll have to go at it different."

Carstairs would have searched on until dark, but he liked Hawthorne, and if the old sheriff had some plan he was willing to play along for the time being.

They rode down off the mountain and turned unhurriedly toward town, coming into the main street in the late afternoon. On the outskirts Hawthorne turned and embarrassment was strong in his manner.

"Reese, I'll have to ask for your gun while you're in town. Whether it's Borden or someone else, I don't want them to have an excuse for a gun play on my street."

Reese let a grunt escape his lips. "Well put,

Sheriff. But I warn you, Duke is not going to steal my ranch."

He held out his gun. Hawthorne took it, shoved it between his belt and his flat stomach, and without speaking again rode ahead, angling off toward the courthouse hill.

Carstairs continued toward the hotel, and was within a block of it when Duke Borden and Mart January turned the corner from the side street, afoot, trailed by the other rider.

Borden saw Reese and stopped abruptly and stood, his big legs spread. He threw back his head arrogantly, hooking his thumbs in the front of his sagging gun belt. His grin and his voice was mocking as he said,

"Captain. I didn't see you in town so I thought you'd left the country."

Reese had brought his horse to a halt. Deliberately he dismounted, led the animal to the nearest hitch rail and hooked the reins over it. Then he faced around. Borden had not moved. Reese walked at him, noting that the two men behind Duke stood watchful, intent, their hands balanced near their holstered guns, expectancy in their eyes.

He kept his voice low, level, fighting it.

"You've been pretty successful, haven't you, Duke?"

Borden's grin widened. "I try to be, Captain. I try."

The answer was still quiet. "But you aren't going to keep the Triple X, Duke. You should know me better than to think I'd let you. Your sniper should have killed me when he killed Alf."

Borden was very certain of himself. He did not even trouble to deny the accusation. It seemed rather to heighten his amusement.

"Too bad. Next time I'll see he shoots straighter."

Reese nodded. "If you want the ranch that badly, do. Because I'll kill you if need be to get it back."

"Try it, Captain. Any time. I always could handle a gun better than you. Why not now?"

Reese could not keep all of the regret from his tone.

"Because I'm not armed now."

He watched the disappointment grow in the huge man's eyes and knew that Borden had hoped to goad him into a fight, to provoke him into facing the three of them. He said tightly, "Take off your gun."

Borden hesitated. He was four inches taller than Reese and thirty pounds heavier. He studied the lined face before him as though to judge how much strength remained in the gaunt body. He cursed. Then he unbuckled his belt and passed it with the holstered gun backward to January.

He charged.

One moment he was standing, the next he was diving for Reese, his big arms extended to encircle the smaller man, to crush him against the barrel chest.

Reese jumped sideways. He caught one of the outstretched wrists, twisting, flipping the big body over his head. Borden rolled across his shoulder and landed with jarring force flat on his back in the hot dust.

Reese waited coldly, watching Borden come to his knees and hands and shake his head. Then he kicked upward at the hanging jaw. Borden's head snapped back and he rolled flat again, groaning.

There was no mercy in Reese. Bitter fury held him and he struck against Nell's marriage, Alf's murder, the stealing of the ranch, all engineered by this man on the ground before him.

He kicked the wide rib cage with all the power behind his worn boot. He reached down, tangled his lean fingers in the thick black hair and hauled Borden partly to his feet, releasing his grip, ramming over a looping blow that broke Borden's nose and sent the man sprawling on his side.

Mart January leaped on Carstairs' back with a savage cry, carrying him forward onto his face, falling on top of him, and Reese flung his head up sharply to crack against January's brow.

Then as Reese struggled to free himself the third rider attacked, slashing his heavy gun barrel along the side of Reese's scalp.

Beneath January, Reese slumped, his nose digging into the street, and felt the gun strike again and yet again. A wicked boot staved against his side. A boot stamped hard on his left hand and pivoted.

He should have been completely out, but the impetus of his rage maintained a spark of consciousness. He was dully aware of shouts from up the street, of his Raiders charging forward.

Borden's man heard them come. He straightened and snapped a shot in their direction, and Whitey Ellis shot him through the head.

Neither January nor Duke Borden made it off the ground, and Whitey Ellis still stood above them slashing Borden wildly across his already bloody face when the sheriff with half the town ran in and pulled him back.

Ellis was beside himself, crying from the sheer intensity of his bursting resentment, writhing to break the grasp of the men who held him.

"Let me go. Let me kill the murdering bastard." The sheriff was bending over Carstairs. He said in relief, "He isn't dead."

Whitey heard. Whitey stopped struggling and turned to see Joe Blunt and Gil Martin lift Carstairs, now unconscious, and start toward the hotel.

Nell and Jenny met them on the porch and Jenny ran ahead of them up the stairs to open the bed.

When the doctor came she had already sponged the blood from the beaten head with cool water. She worked swiftly, deftly, without sound, showing no awareness of the Raiders assembled silent and grim-faced in the hall.

But she was aware of them, feeling and appreciating the bond which knit these men together with a closeness more real than most family ties.

Dr. Dice was a fussy man, thin-haired, with steel-rimmed spectacles. He made small sounds with his tongue and his narrow lips as he examined the welts and gashes where the gun barrel had laid open Carstairs' scalp.

He used his hands with the gentleness of a woman, probing, pushing with his thumbs, hunting fractures. He finished and turned to the girl, shaking his head.

She was at once rigid. "Will he die?"

The doctor lifted his shoulders. "I don't think so. He's got a hard head. Most skulls would have been crushed like an eggshell."

He gave her laudanum, in case the pain became too great, and went away. Whitey Ellis came in to stand beside the bed, to say softly, "I'll stay with him awhile."

She nodded. "I have to get dinner."

She gathered up the soiled towels and hurriedly left the stifling room.

SEVEN

Reese Carstairs knew very little that first night after the fight. He roused twice, once to sense Whitey Ellis sitting silent, bolt upright beside the bed, his shirt wet and plastered against him in the hot motionless air of the lamplighted room. The second time consciousness flickered Nell was in Whitey's chair.

At midmorning he roused more fully and lay staring at the flyspecked ceiling, gripped by a terrible lethargy which made every small movement a thing of torture. Even the weight of the sheet over him was leaden.

In all his troubled life his strength had never been so utterly depleted, and tears brought up by sheer weakness filled his burning eyes.

Sound from the door made him turn his glance that way, and Nell was standing there, a tray on her arm, lovely as he had ever remembered her. She came forward soundlessly, seeing that he was awake, moving the bowl and pitcher from the washstand to the chair and depositing the tray on the stand before she turned her wide, dark gaze on him. Then she bent over him and her whisper was choked.

"Reese, what a terrible thing for Duke to do." He saw that she was crying.

"Oh, my dear." She bent lower, and her mouth was soft and gentle on his bruised lips. "You've been through so much, so very, very much."

He stirred, lacking the strength to draw away from her, resenting this kiss. He wanted her and at the same time was repelled as he sensed her calculated intent.

She saw the reflex. She sat down on the bed and took his scarred hand in both her small ones.

"What can I say to you? How can I explain my shock at having you come back to life after I'd given you up for dead? I was thrown off balance, Reese. I said and did things I didn't mean, but I couldn't stop them. Be a little gentle with me, dear. I, too, have been through a lot in the last few hours, remember."

He saw the tears brim from her eyes and had to fight his desire to pull her into his arms, to comfort her. He sighed deeply, his voice more a breath than a whisper.

"I'm tired, Nell."

At once her manner changed and became brisk. "I'm sorry. I didn't mean to push you now. Here, let me feed you something."

"I'll do that." Jenny was at the doorway, her small face set.

Nell swung to glance at her, then ignoring the words, turned back, arranging the pillows beneath Reese's head, picking up the dish and spooning the warm cereal into his mouth.

Jenny did not move. She stayed in the doorway, making no further comment, no effort to interfere.

Reese ate little, and even that exertion exhausted him. He lay back, turning away his head and closing his eyes.

"He's asleep again," Nell said, and rose.

Jenny stepped aside, waiting for her sister to pass with the tray. Nell hesitated as if unwilling to leave them alone together, and Jenny's low voice was sharp.

"Go ahead."

Nell looked at her for a long moment, then went on into the hall. Jenny followed, her words clear and spaced.

"Leave him alone. You've done enough harm already."

"I'm not doing him any harm. Alf is dead and I need someone, someone stronger than Duke."

"You didn't need him when you ordered him off the ranch."

"I was terribly upset." Nell's tone was suddenly shrill, and the conversation etched through Reese's half sleep like an ugly dream.

"You were upset because he wanted half the ranch, the ranch that is rightfully all his. You wanted to get rid of him quickly. You weren't concerned that he was without money, worn out, that he'd just ridden three thousand miles out of hell. Stay away from him."

"So you can work on him." The older girl laughed shortly.

"Nell, you have a twisted mind."

"And you're so innocent. You've wanted him for years."

Jenny's voice tightened. "I was a little girl when he rode away. I haven't seen him since."

"You had a childish crush on him. You've nursed it all along, always talking about him. Well, you're not going to have him. He's still in love with me."

Nell started down the stairs, then stopped.

"As a matter of fact, Jenny, since I own this hotel, since I am going to live here for the present and since you prefer being a hotelkeeper to having to live with the family, perhaps you'd better mind your manners."

There was a momentary silence, then Jenny spoke, sounding almost amused.

"Are you threatening to deal with me as you did with Reese? Think a minute, Nell, you need me here. This place represents everything you can call your own, even if you bought it with Alf's and Reese's money. And you could never in this world run it alone. But I don't need you. I can take care of myself."

Nell made a choking sound. "Take care of yourself, how? Become a common woman, or marry that rustler, Creed?"

She went on down the stairs, her feet making exclamation points on the hollow uncarpeted treads.

Reese lay staring at the ceiling, sinking finally into another deep sleep. It was evening when he roused again, and Jenny was at the door with his dinner tray.

She came into the soft grayness of the room quietly and put the tray on the stand beside the bed, smiling at him.

"Sleep make you feel any better?"

"Better." He felt strength in him again, but his head and muscles were sore from the pounding.

She told him, "If it helps to know, the doctor had to sew up Duke's cheek where Whitey cut it with his gun sight."

It was no help.

"The judge dismissed the charges against Whitey this afternoon."

Reese looked up quickly. "Charges?"

"He killed one of Duke's men."

"I didn't know."

A small smile touched the corner of her mouth. "The judge was smart. Your Raiders were lined up ready to take the courthouse apart."

He had a picture of his men to make him smile also.

"You're all very close, aren't you? I've been watching. You think of one another before you think of yourselves, and last night when you were hurt they were like wild people. If you had died I know they'd have gone out and burned the ranch and tried to kill everyone on it."

He said warmly, "We've been together a long time, Jenny, and we had to take care of one another to protect ourselves. One after another has been killed, and with each new death those of us who were left drew closer together."

She sighed. "It's good to have such friends. Do you want me to feed you?"

"I think I can manage."

He worked painfully to sit up. His left hand was bandaged where the spike heel had bored almost through his palm, his right had a split knuckle but it could hold a fork.

Jenny cut the meat, mashed the potatoes and added gravy. She watched him eat with increasing appetite, marking it as a further sign of his recovery. When he had finished she reached for the tray.

He put his hand on her arm. "Please stay a minute."

She looked at him inquiringly.

"I overheard you and Nell in the hall this morning."

Color spread lightly in her face. "I thought you were asleep." Her tone was matter-of-fact, without feeling. "Don't let what she said upset you. She was just being Nell."

"What was that about her owning the hotel? Did she buy it to help you?"

"Nell help anyone? Hardly. She bought it as an investment, to build up money of her own and she uses me as she uses everybody else, to further her interests. To be honest, I was glad enough to run it for her. I have little use for my family and I could no longer live at home. Now I'm not certain I'll stay. I'm not certain I can live with her."

His hand slid down and closed over hers. She made no effort to pull away, but her fingers remained still, not responding to his pressure.

"Jenny, do you love me?"

Strain tightened her face and her eyes were guarded, but she kept them level on his.

"My answer could make no difference. You love Nell. You are a very constant man."

He missed her evasion. He missed her tension. "It might make a great deal of difference. I will never fully trust Nell again and I couldn't marry a woman I didn't trust. I have a new life to build, Jenny. . . ." He knew he was blundering but a cloud of weariness blocked his mind. He could only hope she would read his meaning in his eyes.

She surprised him, rising suddenly, pulling her hand free. "Thank you, no. I certainly have no desire to pick you from the arms of another woman no matter how I might feel about you."

She moved as if to leave but he stopped her. "What will you do if you don't stay here?"

"I might marry Ben Creed."

He was startled. "You can't do that. There's still a possibility that Creed had Alf killed."

"I don't believe it. I know Ben Creed as well as anyone in the valley knows him. He went through a lot in the war. He was a prisoner at Andersonville for three years. He hates the South and he hates Southerners. He fought, and he will fight, because Duke and Nell and Alf too were pushing him. But his fight has been an honest one."

She lifted the tray and hurried from the room, leaving Reese with a strange sense of confusion.

He tried to think where he was wrong, but the weight of weariness defeated him. He gave up and surrendered to his body's demand for rest.

In the morning he was up, Whitey Ellis helping him to dress before breakfast was ready, and they met Nell in the lobby as she brought his tray.

A quick frown drew down her brows.

"Reese, the doctor wants you to stay in bed for a week."

He shook his head. "I'm all right. The longer I'm here the longer Duke holds the ranch."

He went on, into the dining room. Nell started to speak to Whitey, but he passed her in silence, and she followed them slowly, going on to the kitchen.

The other five Raiders were already seated, and at the far end of the table Jenny was serving a stranger. She looked up, showing no surprise as Reese came toward her, her manner brisk and efficient. She set down the dishes and straightened.

"You two haven't met. This is Reese Carstairs . . . Ben Creed." She left it there, going into the kitchen.

Carstairs nodded. Creed returned the nod. He made no effort to rise or to shake hands. Reese sat down between Whitey Ellis and Joe Blunt, lowering his head and sidelong studying the man beyond them.

Creed was older than himself by perhaps five years, a big man, strong-faced and self-assured. There was a magnetism about him even before he spoke and Reese felt it would draw an unbiased person into friendship. It would not be this man's way to have ambushed Alf.

Creed looked up and caught Reese's eye and smiled thinly.

"Understand you and Duke had a little trouble. If you have more and need help, let me know."

Carstairs was startled. He raised his head slowly. "I wouldn't have expected the offer from you, not after you jumped the ranch the other night."

Creed shrugged. "I've got no quarrel with you. I don't even know you." His smile turned quizzical. "My fight's with the Triple X trying to grab range that was mine before they showed up here. I cleared the Indians off that range just after the war. Duke Borden's a pusher. Your brother was pretty arrogant, but Duke's worse.

"Whether or not you believe it, I didn't start the shooting. Duke did. He killed two of my men last spring. Claimed they were using a running iron on some Triple X stock.

"Maybe they were. If so, it wasn't under my orders. Now that Duke has the ranch it will get rougher. I'll have to fight harder to live."

Jenny came back with Reese's breakfast and he waited until she had served him, had begun to clear the places of the earlier breakfasts before he asked Creed, "What is it you want?"

There was no hesitation in the quiet answer. "The range north of Cherry Creek between Triple X and me. Duke is trying to squeeze me two ways. His father and brothers are northeast of me, blocking me out of Kings Canyon. The only place I have to grow is a narrow arm northwest, along the Platte. I'm not going to let him haze me into that."

"You don't think I'll do the same when I have the Triple X?" Creed's gaze was direct, calm. There was a certainty, a strength about this man more unsettling than any threat.

"I'd have to find out. But maybe you learned reason during the war, maybe you learned that others have rights, that you have to give as well as take, to live with people."

He finished his coffee, shoved back his chair and rose, looking at the girl who came once more from the kitchen.

"Jenny, can I talk to you in the lobby?"

She nodded, trailing him through the door. Whitey Ellis watched them go, and said in his slow drawl, "There goes a dangerous man. If I were Duke I'd be sort of unhappy quarreling with him."

Reese did not answer. He was unconscious even of the conversation which sprang up among the Raiders now that Creed was gone. They were like that, taciturn and watchful in the presence of strangers, talking easily only among themselves.

He was aware of nothing except that Jenny had gone with Creed, and that it was of importance to him. He tried to analyze the reaction. He had been away from women for a long time. He had never known his mother and his stepmother had shown him only antagonism. Nell alone had he ever felt that he knew, had he ever wanted to marry, yet under this new emotion he wondered if his love for her had not perhaps been bred of association, a cultured love rather than genuine.

He glanced at Joe Blunt, at Whitey, and rose, going with haste he did not intend toward the lobby. Creed was gone, and he felt an inexplicable relief.

He crossed to the girl as she turned from the doorway, and saw the color rise in her cheeks as if she read his eyes, but her voice was casual.

"What did you think of him?"

He knew the impulse to take her shoulders, to feel their softness under his hands. He did not, but his voice deepened with his effort to control his answer.

"The important point is what you think of him. Was he asking you to marry him just now?"

Her color heightened. Her head came up.

"I don't think you have the right to ask me that."

"I have to. If Nell was right . . . you can't love two men. You can't marry Creed."

"You would try to stop me?" Defiance edged her tone.

"I'd ask you to marry me. We could build a good life at the ranch."

She stared at him, incredulous. "You don't seriously mean that?"

"Why not?"

"Two days ago you were heartbroken because the woman you loved had married your brother. What are you trying to do, revenge the hurt Nell gave you by using me to flaunt as your wife?"

Her scorn made him suddenly curt. "The idea had not occurred to me."

"Then what has? You certainly won't stand there and tell me that from being in love with one woman all your life you can about-face and love another between suns?

"I'm sorry. I can't accept that. Either you are trying to hit back at Nell and salve your own injured vanity or it's pity. I can't take pity, if that's your reason. I think I will marry Ben Creed. At least I'll go to the dance with him, which is what he just asked me. I told him no. I've changed my mind."

She turned and hurried toward the kitchen, her small body rigid.

EIGHT

As she left the lobby the raiders came from the dining room, looking more rested and relaxed than Reese could remember.

He crossed to them, stopping before Joe Blunt, his clipped words a direct order.

"Get the gear together. We're moving on."

The men swung, startled, not believing, dismay and dying hope mingling in their eyes. Their faces were curiously marked, white where the heavy beards had kept off the sun, the foreheads and noses burned to a deep mahogany.

Joe Blunt said, "Why?"

Reese showed a rare irritation with his sergeant, "We can't sit here forever living off that girl."

"But where will we go?" It was Bo Martin, his soft Cajun accent as forlorn as Reese had ever heard it.

"We'll find a place."

"And what will we eat?"

Reese's harassed expression changed, his mouth setting in a hard line.

"According to Alf there are over five thousand cows here wearing my brand. We won't lack for meat. As for the rest, I'll talk to the storekeeper."

He moved off, out of the lobby, leaving a strained silence behind him.

Moose Kobbler and Pete Mullins were alone when Reese walked into the dim store. The ex-cook grinned warmly at Reese's greeting but the storekeeper's manner was neutral as Reese came to the counter.

"What can I do for you?"

Reese was already stretching, drawing his flat stomach flatter to dig deep in his trousers pocket, to pull out a small package carefully wrapped in a bandanna handkerchief.

He opened it on the counter, exposing a folded sheaf of peso notes, translucent with sweat. This was money he had taken from the Mexican general's house when the rebels had captured the place and freed the Raiders. It was the only money he had had since Maximilian's fall.

"Two of these are worth an American dollar below the line," he said. "Can I buy some supplies with them?"

Kobbler looked down at the money without enthusiasm.

"I don't know what I'd do with it."

"You can send it to a bank in Denver," Reese told him. "It must have some rate of exchange. I'll leave it all with you. If you get more for it than the value of what I take you can credit my account."

Slowly the storekeeper touched the bills with a white forefinger, then picked them up, examining them critically, noting how limp they were, how wrinkled. He nodded.

"What supplies do you want?"

Reese began his list with a sack of flour, of coffee, of beans, and ended it with ammunition, watching as Kobbler wrote it down and adding, "Don't suppose there's a wagon in town I can borrow?"

The storekeeper hesitated again, then shrugged, and met Pete's triumphant look. "So you were right, he's staying."

Kobbler waved a hand, indicating the rear of the building.

"I got a wagon, and there's a team out back."

Reese thanked him. He left the coolness of the store and found his men waiting dispiritedly in the street before the hotel. He sent the Martins for Kobbler's horses, and with the others carried the supplies to the wagon.

Austin and the Martins began loading, Joe Blunt, Whitey Ellis and Pop Greer went for the Raiders' horses, and Reese returned to the hotel.

Jenny and Nell met him in the lobby and Nell stepped quickly forward.

"Whitey Ellis took all your things from the room. You're not going with them?"

He looked toward Jenny but she avoided his eyes. He said, "We couldn't continue to impose ourselves here, Nell."

"Where are you going? I thought you were going to make Duke give back the ranch."

His smile was thin. "I am. We'll make a camp in the hills. When we're settled I'll be back."

He turned to Jenny, going to her. "I've no way now to thank you for what you've done."

She was forced to look up at him, but her eyes told nothing.

"No thanks are necessary," she said in a low voice.

"I'll make it up to you some way, some day."

She only shook her head.

Dissatisfied he pivoted and went back to the Raiders.

The site they found lay in the mouth of a small canyon where the waters of the Michigan rushed out of the hills and from there wound sedately across the valley floor. A jutting finger of the mountain behind partially cut off a little meadow, perhaps an acre and a half of lush, knee-deep grass for the horses.

They chose the place and began setting up the camp with the unconscious ease of men who live in the open. They felt better here, less wary, and even Reese found a smile, breathing the astringent air, feeling suddenly that he was a part of this verdant land.

Joe Blunt stood beside him, silent, listening,

absorbing into himself all of the things he might need to know about this location.

"Take over," Reese told him. "Whitey and I are running the wagon back to town."

Ellis looked at him. "I could do that alone."

"I want to talk to the court, to the judge."

Ellis scratched his head beneath his hat-band. "I don't think that'll do any good."

"Maybe not. I've got to try."

Reese turned back to Blunt. "After you build a corral, better throw up some kind of a lean-to. It rains in this country. Then find a Triple X steer and butcher it out."

Blunt's bulldog face was expressionless. "And if we run into some of Duke's crew?"

"Use your own judgment," Reese said.

It was better than a half-hour drive back to town and Ellis drove without speaking, honoring Reese's silence as the only privacy available to men who lived so closely. He dropped Reese at the hotel and went to return the borrowed rig.

The lobby was deserted, but Reese heard the children in the kitchen and went toward the sounds, finding Nell and Jenny at the sink, preparing vegetables for the evening meal.

Both looked around, showing surprise that he was back so quickly, then Jenny dropped her eyes again to her task.

Reese spoke to Nell. "Walk over to the

courthouse with me?"

Nell took off her apron. "If Jenny will look after the children."

She did not wait for the answer. Whitey Ellis was coming up the porch steps as they came through the door. He turned and trailed after them.

Reese told him, "No need for you to come."

Ellis' voice was easy. "Long as there's a chance of meeting Borden's crew, I'm not leaving you alone."

They climbed the short grade, feeling the warmth of the exertion mingled with the heat of the day. The courtroom was empty, and they went downstairs to Hawthorne's office.

The sheriff was talking with a deputy but he broke off, nodding to Nell, his face lighting as Reese came in. It was apparent he had a genuine liking for Reese Carstairs.

"What are you doing out of bed?"

Nell stepped forward. "He wouldn't stay down. He's even moved."

"We were eating the hotel into bankruptcy," Reese smiled. "We're up in the canyon a ways. Know where I might find the judge?"

Hawthorne reached up to pull on his chin. "That's kind of hard to figure. There's no court in the afternoon. I'd say probably over at Gover's bar. Around the corner from the hotel."

They thanked him and left and outside the bar Nell waited with Whitey Ellis while Reese went in.

Reese crossed the shadowed room, stopping at the bar, asking for the judge. The bartender was sleepy, endlessly polishing a glass. At Reese's question he pointed with the glass toward a rear table where five men played a lackadaisical game of poker.

"Sittin' against the wall."

Reese batted at a blowfly which buzzed across his eyes, going on to the table, realizing that he did not know the judge's name.

"I'm Reese Carstairs," he said. "My brother's widow is outside. Could we talk to you?"

The judge glanced up, nodded. "Soon as we finish this hand." He played on. He won a small pot, picked up his money and rose, taking time to put on the coat from the back of his chair.

Reese watched, appraising him, a soft-looking man in his mid-fifties, heavy set, his actions slow, deliberate, his gray eyes withdrawn.

"I know why you're here," he said as they came toward the door. "I could have saved you the time and trouble. I drew Alf's will."

He shouldered the door open and stepped out and Nell moved toward him smiling.

"Judge Burke. How good of you. Let's go over to my hotel."

Burke had a courtly manner with women. He offered Nell his arm, and the four of them made a small parade, around the corner, up the steps to the gallery. Burke seated Nell in a cane-bottom chair, then turned inquiringly to Reese.

"You've read the will, of course. Do you recall the last paragraph?"

There was no emotion in Reese's face. "Judge Burke," he said, "under that will, Nell is afraid for the life of her son. My brother has already been murdered. I don't believe this is what Alf intended."

Burke took a moment to sit down beside Nell, to rub his plump hand across his red face.

"True. True. I tried to tell Alf. You Texans are bullheaded, you know. The trouble is that the intent of the testator and what he puts on paper are not always in accord. Duke has done nothing that violates the written provisions of the will.

"And I have no power to set it aside. Borden could appeal any decision of mine to the territorial courts. I would certainly be overruled. Hawthorne has told me of your suspicions but there's nothing I know of that you can do except surrender, unless you can prove Duke murdered Alf. I had a great admiration for your brother. If you can substantiate your charge, we might have a chance. Otherwise, as a judge appointed by the Federal Government to this district I have no option but to uphold Duke's claim."

Nell gasped and leaned forward to protest but Reese put a hand on her arm.

"We'll have to find another way," he said. "It isn't Burke's fault."

NINE

The judge was gone. Whitey Ellis sat on the porch rail, Reese remained standing, and Nell sat bowed in her chair.

Her voice was filled with bitterness as she said, "Why did I ever believe Duke? Why did I let Alf keep him on the ranch?"

Reese made no attempt to answer.

"Let me take the boys and settle this," Whitey said tightly.

Nell drew a long tortured breath, very close to a sob.

"I wish you'd never given Alf that bill of sale. Without it he could never have written that will. I almost tore it up this morning."

Suddenly Reese was alert. "You still have it? Didn't Alf register it in Texas?"

She looked up in bewilderment. "Was he supposed to register it?"

Reese laughed. The laughter came from deep within him and would not stop. Finally he managed to speak.

"To be legally his, the brand must be registered in Alf's name, and the bill of sale must accompany the registration. If it isn't registered, Alf never owned the Triple X. Duke couldn't inherit it from him. Go get that bill of sale, Nell."

The girl rose and nearly ran inside, barely avoiding Jenny who came from the dining room with Lin at her heels.

"Nell," she said. "What's happened?"

Nell almost shouted from the stairs, "Duke doesn't own the ranch. It belongs to Reese."

She went on, taking the stairs two at a time and Jenny watched her out of sight, then walked slowly forward onto the gallery.

"What did she mean?"

Reese was grinning. He told her about Alf's neglecting to register the bill of sale.

"But the ranch was in Alf's name. He filed on it."

"How many acres?"

She did not know.

Nell was hurrying back through the lobby, hearing Reese's question.

"Six hundred and forty." She sounded jubilant.

"And the rest is public graze." It was Reese. "Under Alf's will all Borden owns is half of the home buildings and the six hundred and forty acres. The rest of the range is public land. The Triple X brand and the cattle that wear it are mine."

He took the paper from Nell, unable to

control its slight tremble as he held it. He remembered so clearly the morning he had written it. He had used the back of a government order which had been in his pocket. He turned it over, reading the Spanish with a sense of unreality. It was the order by which Maximilian had given him command of the personal bodyguard.

Slowly he began to tear it, until nothing but shreds of paper filled his fingers. Whitey held out a sulphur match and Reese struck it, lighting the fragments, letting each fall to the gallery floor as it took fire.

When the last had fallen, he said,

"Wait here," and sidestepped the child, Lin, to go down the steps.

Judge Burke was again in the poker game. He looked up as Reese came forward.

"Sit in."

Reese shook his head. "Can I bother you again?"

The judge glanced at his cards. He shrugged.

"The way these have run since I came back I should have stayed with you anyhow."

He threw the hand on the table and rose. At the door he said, "What's on your mind now?"

Reese wished he could have taken the man to the bar. He had no money. Instead he stepped him into the shade of the wooden awning.

"What if I told you Alf never owned the Triple X brand, that every cow wearing it is mine?"

Burke's eyes widened. "What kind of a game is this?"

"No game." Reese said it shortly, and explained the unregistered bill of sale. "Originally the Texas ranch belonged to my mother's father. It came to me at his death. It never belonged to my father at all, nor to Alf, since he was only a half brother."

Burke looked at him with narrowed eyes. Reese went on.

"As far as the Texas records show the cattle are still mine. Duke Borden can have the buildings and the six forty. The graze is government land anyhow."

Unexpectedly Burke laughed. "And he only owns half of the ranch at that. I want to see Duke's face when he hears this."

Reese was abruptly sober. "I don't want him to hear it until we can straighten it out. What do I need in the way of proof?"

"The records from Texas."

"I'll start a man after them tonight. Thanks."

He left the judge and gained the corner of the main street. He stopped. Before the hotel stood two horses other than his and Whitey's, and their deeply burned brands read Triple X.

He glanced quickly along the street and saw no one, and started on a long lope for the hotel. He took the porch steps in a flying leap, looking ahead through the lobby door, seeing Duke Borden's back, broad, powerful, the shoulders hunched in anger, before Nell, hearing Nell's voice shrill with vindictiveness. He was too late.

"Weren't you so very clever? You stole a ranch. But the cattle weren't Alf's to will you. They still belong to Reese. Alf never registered the bill of sale. Laugh about that, my greedy brother."

Reese stopped in the doorway, scanning the lobby quickly. Whitey Ellis lounged against the far wall, his eyes alert and watchful. Mart January stood at Borden's elbow. Jenny clutched the children against her, tense.

Hearing him they turned, and Borden's eyes were black with fury.

"Try to take one single cow, Captain. Just try."

Reese steadied his breathing. "You're whipped, Duke." Borden walked at him. Reese had a choice of stepping aside or blocking the bigger man. His impulse was to slash his fist into Duke's face. He curbed it. He did not intend to start a fight in the narrow confines of the room, with the children underfoot, with the women present. He stepped aside and Borden passed him, January coming from his place to follow Duke.

Reese watched as they mounted and rode

up the street, then wheeled back into the room, speaking to Whitey,

"Let's head for camp. You're leaving for Texas tonight."

TEN

The habit of decision was strong in Jenny Borden. Her childhood in Texas had been cut short by war and her young mind had early appraised her shiftless parents, her grasping brothers and sisters, deciding that her life would have to be shaped by her own judgment.

Yet there was no decision in her now as she stood before the crazed mirror in its dark oval frame and dressed for the dance. Her fingers fumbled at the hooks and eyes of the soft pink chambray dress, her thoughts were sober, searching out some solution to her problems.

Reese Carstairs had hurt her in asking her to marry him. Her first reaction had been that he was trying to spite Nell and it was only much later that reason had overcome her anger.

Reese was not mean. She was sure the war years could not have so changed the boy on whom she had had her first crush. Still she was equally sure that he could not have fallen out of love with Nell and into love with her so abruptly. The proposal then must have been an honest one, made in concern for her, his way of offering help.

She felt a wave of shame that she had misunderstood, sensing now that his weariness, his harassment, had made him clumsy. She would have to make amends, but carefully so he would not also misunderstand. She would not marry Reese out of expediency, that was one decision she could make. These thoughts brought her to the consideration of her own need of help.

She had to leave the hotel. She knew she and her sister could not again live under the same roof. She would have to find another job. It did not occur to her to look for someone to lean upon.

She shook her head suddenly, putting away the troublesome questions, giving a final pat to the dark braid which haloed her small head and catching up the light shawl from the bed, determined to enjoy her evening.

Ben Creed would be waiting in the lobby, impatient that she was late. Yet the lateness was unavoidable. The more remote ranchers and miners would spend the night in town after the dance and both Jenny and Nell had been busy long after supper caring for the full house.

She went out through the tiny sitting room and the dimly lighted hall and descended the stairs, her step light on the spur-worn treads.

The lobby doors stood open to the warm night air, showing her Ben Creed's restless figure pacing the gallery, the crooked stogie clamped in his teeth glowing like a firefly in the darkness.

Below her, near the registration desk sat Nell, her head bent above the boy's shirt on her lap, mending by the insufficient light of the desk lamp. The effect, Jenny knew, was calculated to compare herself still laboring at domestic chores against a carefree sister running off to play.

Nell, she thought, actually believed she was being imposed upon, not considering that the children whose care kept her from the dance were hers, forgetting that their father was so recently dead.

She forced a cheerful good night and hurried on, ignoring Nell's deep-drawn sigh and murmured "Have a good time."

On the gallery she accepted Ben's arm, glad for his firm grasp and moved with him down the steps to turn toward the long lodge hall.

Music drifted to them. Moonlight silvered the dusty street and softened the rough bark of the log buildings they passed. She felt that she should be content, happy and at peace, but was not.

Instead she was acutely conscious of Ben Creed and for the first time aware of the similarities existing between him and Reese Carstairs. Both were direct men, tempered rather than embittered by their hardships which could have corroded a lesser man's strength.

Questioning herself she knew that this man's magnetism had drawn her toward him from the first. Why then had she not married him during the past year? What instinct held her back? It had nothing to do with Reese. She had believed him dead for a long while and her girlhood worship of him would certainly not have kept her from taking another husband.

Creed's voice came softly as if he were following her thoughts.

"Jenny, you said you'd have an answer for me soon."

She stopped short, and indecision ran through her again. She lifted her eyes to his. Her voice was honest, the words distinct.

"I won't lie to you, Ben. I thought I would have an answer. I don't. And I don't know how soon I will have. I'm more confused than I've ever been in my life."

"Can you tell me about it?"

She shook her head. "I'm sorry."

He said evenly, "Take your time. I've had a deal of practice at waiting."

Her quick smile thanked him and she moved on, not wanting to think any more tonight.

Voices reached them from inside the hall, the scrape of shuffling feet and the hoarse rhythm of the caller above the shrill fiddles.

They came in to find laughing groups filling the benches which lined the rough-hewn walls of the long, narrow, crowded room and at the far end saw the musicians and Sheriff Hawthorne on the raised platform. Hawthorne was already hot, his shirt sweated as he swung his arms and stamped his feet, shouting directions to the dancers.

Three squares occupied the floor, men in store pants, girls in bright ginghams swirling, weaving, swinging through the intricate patterns.

Creed turned Jenny along the side, back toward the refreshment corner, pausing as they met friends, talking a moment with the doctor. The gaiety lifted Jenny's mood, the heavy thoughts of the day left her and she smiled up at her escort as he pulled her toward a new forming square.

It was an hour later when they dropped out to work through the panting crowd for a cooling cup of punch. Jenny loved to dance and she stood swaying, flushed and laughing, watching as Hawthorne called a grand right and left. She felt Creed's eyes on her appreciatively and automatically tucked up the tendril of dark hair that had escaped to curl at the nape of her slim neck, and then beyond him she saw Reese Carstairs coming toward them along the side aisle.

She stiffened and Creed, seeing the movement, turned and nodded as the other man reached them. Reese returned the nod and smiled uncertainly at the girl.

Jenny spoke too quickly, uncomfortable again with these two men together.

"Reese. I thought you'd gone back to the camp."

"I did," he said. "I came in again with Whitey. He started for Texas right after dark. Then I stopped at the hotel. Nell said you were here." He looked up, around the noisy, playful scene and then at Creed.

"It's a long time since I went to a dance. With your permission I'll ask Jenny."

Creed's agreeing smile was automatic, brief, and Jenny felt the color come up stronger in her face.

"Thanks, but I'm so warm." She turned to Creed, holding out her cup. "May I have some more punch?"

"I'll get it for you," he said, and moved off.

Reese watched him go then looked at the girl. "I'm sorry you won't dance with me, Jenny."

"Not right now, Reese, please," she said, surprised at her quick fear of being so close to him.

His tone was gentle, insistent, kept low so that others nearby would not hear his words.

"Jenny, forgive me. I had no right to ask you to marry me under the circumstances and certainly no right to question you about Ben Creed."

She had recovered herself and was glad the subject was in the open. "It's all right, Reese," she said. "I think I understand now. And I said things I shouldn't have, too. Let's forget it. Of course I'll dance with you." Suddenly she giggled. "After I drink the punch I didn't really want."

They were laughing easily together when Creed came back. The man pushed his way toward them, alert, watching to judge the relationship between these two, but he said nothing as Reese took the girl onto the dance floor.

Reese was awkward at first, but the stiffness relaxed as the music brought out the long-forgotten rhythm of the steps and Jenny felt a tug of sympathy, knowing the time that must have passed since he had danced. She saw the enjoyment rise slowly in him and was glad, remembering the carefree spirit of the boy who had ridden away to war.

Hawthorne saw them and waved, and bawled a new turn, "Swing your partners, now you men . . ." and Reese grinned widely and lifted the girl in a high circling arc that took her breath.

He brought her down lightly, then swerved to miss bumping a group of watching men, and she felt him tense as his eye ran over them. They were ranch hands, in high spirits, already drunk, as much with this noisy break in the monotony of their lives as with whiskey, eager to have a part in the excitement.

As she caught her balance, the nearest hand leaped between her and Reese, wrapping his arm about her and pulling her against him.

Before she could speak Reese had grabbed the man's shoulder and spun him. She saw him relax, his eyes change as he saw the young face.

He said only, "Wait your turn, son."

But the boy was feeling big. He swung on Reese, a heavy smash to the cheek which caught Reese unprepared and staggered him backward into the others.

Jenny knew these men and the wildness within them, and ducked away. The riders yelled, delighted at this chance for a battle, caught Reese and pitched him forward against the edge of the stage.

At least one fight was inevitable at any dance, was a part of the fun for these healthy young animals, but the girl was worried for Reese, still battered from his fight with Duke. She stayed near the fore as women scattered and men shuffled back to clear a space.

Reese had hardly turned before the group was on him, outmatching him by their youth and numbers, but suddenly Ben Creed was at his side. She saw their glances meet, and then in reluctant admiration watched their skill.

Fighting was a science with both these men, learned in a hard school where life, not rowdy acclaim, was the goal. They fought silently, carefully, sure of each movement, and their experience told clearly against the wild swings of the drunken attackers.

It was over quickly, the riders quitting, happy with the violence whether they won or lost and she heard Hawthorne calling for a new set, heard the fiddles pick up their interrupted strain as Reese and Creed came toward her.

Reese, she thought, had found no pleasure in the fight and his voice was apologetic as he said, "I guess I'll have to learn to dance again, Jenny. I haven't been in a thing like that for years."

Creed's laugh was easy. "Nor I. I'm glad there were two of us. These young bucks wear me out."

But another thought was in Jenny's mind.

"Ben," she said, "there's not a Triple X man here. If there were he'd have been in the middle of the fight. What does it mean?"

Creed looked around, at once alert. "You're right. I don't like it. I'd better head for the ranch." He turned, starting for the door, calling back to Reese, "Carstairs, will you see her home?"

Reese hesitated, taking her arm. "Stay with Hawthorne, will you? I'll ride with Creed."

Then he was gone, trailing the rancher.

They hadn't reached the doorway when it was blocked by another figure, gesturing, yelling to be heard above the din.

Behind her, Jenny heard Hawthorne order the music stopped, and the voice came loud across the suddenly quiet room.

"There's a wounded man in the trail, maybe three miles out. I was afraid to bring him in without a wagon."

Hawthorne jumped heavily from the stage, shouldering through the crowd with Jenny at his heels, passing Creed and Reese to stop before the newcomer.

"Who is he?" It was Hawthorne.

"Never saw him before. He looks young but his hair's nearly white. . . ."

Premonition struck at Jenny and Reese was beside the man in one long stride. "Is he wearing an old Confederate jacket?"

The man nodded. "Know him?"

"Whitey."

The girl and Reese said it together and Reese's voice was a groan. "Get the doctor. Get a wagon."

Dr. Dice was already moving forward, and Jenny stepped before Reese, commanding his attention.

"Bring him to the hotel. You can't take care of a badly wounded man in the hills."

He nodded but his eyes weren't seeing her and she could only hope he had heard her words as he ran from the hall.

ELEVEN

Whitey lay in a bend of the trail where it looped around the base of a timbered hogback. Reese Carstairs reached him first, dropping from his horse to kneel beside the figure, certain from its stillness that the man was dead.

A moment later the doctor thrust him aside, reaching for the pulse and then looking up to say, "He's alive," and tearing open the bloody shirt, exposing the purple-edged hole, running his hand beneath Whitey's back.

The hand came out bloody. "Heavy caliber. Bullet went clean through," Dr. Dice went on, talking more to himself than to the others.

Hawthorne made a low sound in his throat.

The doctor finished his emergency bandaging as the wagon racketed up, then supervised as they gently lifted the limp figure onto the blankets in its bed.

Reese rode the rig back to town, cradling Whitey in his lap, feeling the pain as if it were his own each time the slow turning wheels jarred against a rock, his lips pressed tight against his fear.

It was not fear of Duke Borden or his men, but with the loss of each Raider, something was whittled from him and he feared death now. So many others killed, Alf murdered and Whitey . . .

"But not Whitey," he said and knew that he said it aloud.

In town the sidewalk was lined with the curious. Music from the hall told that the dance still continued but the lateness of the hour was drawing off the more sober citizens of Walden.

The wagon stopped before the hotel and strong hands reached up to help Reese carry Whitey inside. He had a moment of surprise that it was Creed and then remembered that he had vaguely realized Creed had ridden with them to find the wounded man instead of going to his home.

Jenny had prepared her own room, since the revelers had taken all the others, and now ran up the steps to show them the way. They laid Whitey on her bed and the doctor shooed them out, busying himself with undressing his patient and muttering to himself, unintelligible sounds of disapproval.

Jenny took Reese and Creed into her small sitting room and put her hands on Carstairs' shoulders, shaking him a little, trying to penetrate his daze.

"Shouldn't the Raiders be told?"

He looked at her, his mind dulled by shock and a gnawing anger. It seemed to him that he had lived with this anger all of his life and the name Duke Borden burned like a fire within him. He did not hear the girl's words, nor Creed's as the rancher turned away, saying, "I'll ride out for them."

The doctor came to the door, calling impatiently for hot water, and Jenny and Nell hurried out and back, coming and going with water, towels, bandages. Reese slumped into a corner chair, helpless in this bustle, his mind slowly revolving around Whitey and Borden. He was hardly aware when the doctor sent the girls from the inner room, when they came to sit silently and wait.

It was Nell who broke the long silence, coming across to lay her small hand on his where it rested on his knee.

"Reese, what about the records from Texas now?"

He looked up, his face empty, unseeing, and shook his head.

"I don't know. Wait until . . ." he broke off, his eyes going again to the bedroom door.

Nell went on, insistence coming into her tone.

"I know you're only thinking about Whitey tonight. I don't blame you for that, but the more time Duke has . . . I'm afraid."

Annoyance made him frown and pulled his thoughts to what she was saying.

"You've nothing to fear now, Nell," he told her. "You're no threat to Duke any longer, nor is your son. I'll get the records. And I'll keep my promise to Alf. You and the children will share as partners in the cattle."

A sigh escaped her as if she had needed this reassurance. She patted Reese's shoulder and, avoiding looking at Jenny, moved out of the room.

Reese did not watch her leave, but his mouth twisted and Jenny, reading the violence of his expression, said softly, "If you're thinking of Duke, Reese, please don't you go after him."

Her words startled him, his eyes met hers and she leaned forward to hold this momentary attention.

"I'm not protecting Duke. I'm not even trying to protect you. I'm asking you to keep on the way you've started, use the law to get your rights."

He gave her no answer and she said no more, only moving her chair to sit nearer him. He looked at her face and saw the smudged circles beneath her dark eyes and sensed her weariness, yet knew that she would wait with him and was made warmer by her presence.

The wait was long. It was almost dawn when Dr. Dice came from Whitey's bedside.

"Near thing," he told them. "But he lived through the wagon ride. He's still alive — he's got a chance. I'll be back."

Carstairs and Jenny had come automatically to their feet and as the doctor bustled by them, out through the door, Reese sat down again abruptly, his legs unwilling to support him.

Jenny stepped close, folding her arms about him, drawing his head against her breasts and holding him quietly.

He rested there a few minutes and then straightened and rose again, looking down into her upturned, searching eyes. His arms went around her, his lips found hers, and demand came sharply alive between them.

The sound of booted feet in the hall broke through the moment, and when Ben Creed appeared in the doorway ahead of the Raiders, the two stood apart. But their awareness of each other was yet so intense that it struck Creed like a blow, robbing the rancher of words.

Unnoting, the Raiders crowded past him, forming their old tight group around their captain, their eyes asking their wordless question.

"He's got a chance," Reese said, and went before them into the bedroom.

Jenny stayed where she was, unwilling to trespass on their closeness, and did not see Creed's searching study of her.

Beyond the closed door Whitey's breathing was shallow, uneven, the only sound in the room as the men stood above him, their heads bent, avoiding one another's eyes.

It was Pop Greer who said, finally, "One of us has to get to Texas and that'll be me. You gotta stay, Captain, and you'll need the rest of them here."

Pop Greer was older, not quite so fast in a fight as he had been, knowing where his usefulness lay.

Joe Blunt said flatly, "Austin, you and the Martins ride with Pop to the Denver stagecoach. I'll stay here with the captain."

Reese Carstairs' protest died on his lips. No order now would make these men leave him and Whitey alone here.

TWELVE

Ben Creed rode in taciturn silence, passing no word to any of the three riders who followed him, the rhythmic clink of their harness trappings the only sound of their progress. The deep grass muffled the horses' running hoofbeats and the crushed blades released their rich odor.

In this country Creed no longer rode alone, knowing that he was in constant danger from Duke Borden's men and exercising the trained caution of an experienced soldier rather than giving way to the rebellion, the bravado that had long been his weakness.

It was an irksome practice and kept his temper short. But Creed had become a careful man, a man with a plan for his future and he had no intention of being taken unaware by such a fool as Borden.

Instead of following the trail where it climbed the bench to skirt the heavy timber, he made a sweeping detour across the open meadowland. Alf Carstairs had died from a sniper's bullet at that spot and Borden was unimaginative enough to use the place a second time.

But Creed did not mean to die for a long while yet. He had come into this country shortly after the war, fought the Indians for his ranch and his success had been more owing to his own resourcefulness than to any help from the Army.

Before the war, before Andersonville, an inner violence had led him to many mistakes, mistakes so costly that they had once wiped out everything he had. Steel within him had kept him alive through the long prison years, and the very need to survive had taught him control.

He felt the gnawing urge of the violence now, thinking about the girl and Carstairs. Had it not been for Jenny, Carstairs would have been a man worth friendship. Creed had recognized in the other a toughness akin to his own, restrained and developed into strength through years in prison. But everything the rancher had was invested in three things: the cattle, the land, and most important, the girl. These he would never give up and at least Carstairs was a man worth fighting.

The intensity of his feeling escaped him in a low sound, and Clem Davis pulled up beside him.

"What is it?"

The question was a trigger and Creed lashed out, bitter words with no meaning, then caught himself and said in a calmer tone, "Just thinking."

Davis was his foreman, hard as Creed himself but without Creed's foresight and drive. Creed scorned him as he scorned all of his riders. He had chosen them carefully, a tough crew but not outlaws. Gunfighters they were, men who obeyed any order for pay.

Creed paid them well, and stood apart, a lone man, silent, asking no one's counsel, making his careful plans and directing their development with the cold precision of a strategist.

He looked around at his men as he led them back into the trail and past the Triple X lane. In his present mood he would have been almost glad for a challenge from Duke no matter how many riders Borden had at his call, but they saw no one and went on at a swinging gait which ate up the six miles between the two ranch houses.

Creed's home ranch was built farther off the main road than Carstairs', fortlike log buildings with narrow slit windows which had first served as loopholes against Indian attack.

They rode to the corral and dismounted, and Creed motioned Clem Davis into the house with him.

Inside, the front room was littered with

gear, but not dirty, for Creed's years in Andersonville had left in him a loathing for the filth he had known there. Here his Chinese cook spent more effort than most women in caring for the house.

Creed pushed aside a crate of new books and sat on a corner of the plank table, while Davis waited near the door for orders.

Without preamble Creed said, "I want to know everything that happens on the Triple X from now on. Keep a lookout in the brush up on the bench above them. Change them, keep them fresh so they don't miss anything. And warn the entire crew, I don't want Duke to know he's being watched."

Davis could not restrain the curiosity that rose in his hawklike face, and Creed, seeing it, broke his habit to explain the order.

"Carstairs claims the cattle belong to him, that they never were Alf's. Whitey Ellis was on his way to Texas for the proof when he was bushwhacked. That was a stupid move on Duke's part, Carstairs has already sent another man.

"Borden will know it today or tomorrow and he'll make another try. I'm guessing he'll want to get rid of the cattle, sell them before Carstairs can claim them legally."

Davis shrugged, grinning, and for one of the few times since he began working for Creed, volunteered an opinion.

"Sounds good. Without cows Duke won't

be crowding you off the range. If I were you I'd help him."

"You aren't me," said Creed. He did not explain further the plan already roughed out in his mind.

He reacted quickly to threat, had always had the ability to conceive a master plan. By now he had developed the patience to wait and alter the framework to fit the changing actions of other people involved.

Duke Borden, he had decided, must kill Reese Carstairs and he, Creed, must be fighting on Carstairs' side at the time. He did not know yet how deep an attachment existed between Carstairs and Jenny, but he would not chance the possibility of the girl marrying Reese. Thus Carstairs must die, and in dying leave Jenny grateful to Creed for the stand he had taken. Gratitude would set up the proper situation, allowing him to win Jenny.

To Davis he said, "As soon as you see that Borden is gathering any stock, send a man to town for me."

Davis was startled. "But you just came from town. You going back?"

"That's right." Creed's tone was short, shutting off further comment.

He rose and went into the bedroom, saddle-rolling half a dozen clean shirts and socks.

On a fresh horse he turned into the brush

behind the ranch buildings, rather than taking the trail. He did not want to weaken his crew for this ride, in case Borden panicked and chose to attack the BC ranch, yet caution made him seek the protection of the timber.

He was in no hurry, yet he had no desire to leave Reese a free field with the girl during the days that Whitey's illness would keep Carstairs at the hotel.

He rode slowly, picking the easiest path, making one detour behind the Triple X to dismount and work a cautious way down to timber edge for a long studying look at the activity below. Then he returned to his horse and continued into town.

Jenny Borden looked up in surprise as he entered the lobby.

"What are you doing back here?"

He had no easy answer. "I got to thinking. Carstairs' men all rode to Denver. Duke's sure to find out and maybe come gunning."

Her dark eyes warmed and impulsively she reached across the desk to touch his hand.

"I knew you liked him — the way you jumped in and helped in the fight last night."

Creed nodded, not pushing it. Whatever he might have found in Carstairs under other circumstances, nothing would swerve him from his present intent.

"Where is he?"

"With Whitey. He slept a little this

morning but he's been up there ever since. Those two are closer than brothers."

"Have you a room for me?" He grinned.

"Quit teasing," she smiled back at him. "Aside from dance nights when do we have more than a couple of drummers in the place?"

She reached a key from the rack and led Creed up the stairs, to the room at the end of the hall. Coming back she stopped at her own door.

Reese was slumped in the chair beside the bed and she thought he was asleep, but as she was about to retreat he stirred and opened his eyes, smiling automatically at sight of her.

She looked toward Whitey, his figure still as death.

"How is he?"

Carstairs' shrug was more expressive than any words. "He was conscious a while ago. I think he's out of the coma, just sleeping now. At least he's alive and at noon the doctor said if he made it through the day his chances would be better."

He rose, stretching his cramped muscles. "Have you had any rest today?"

She nodded. "I had a nap. Supper will be ready in a few minutes and Ben Creed just rode in."

"Creed? I thought he was worried about his ranch."

"He left his crew there. He got to thinking that Duke might ride in here so he came back to help you if necessary. He's in the room at the end of the hall."

Reese Carstairs felt that his drugged brain was missing her meaning somehow. Why should Creed come here to help him? It did not fit with his impression of the man. Yet he had fought at his side once, and ridden with him for Whitey when he should have been looking out for his own ranch. Carstairs' years of trouble had taught him not to trust anyone fully save his Raiders and he could not name any reason for Creed's apparent friendship, unless it were to impress Jenny.

He followed her thoughtfully into the hall as Creed came from his own room, raising his hand in a wordless salute, and together they descended to the dining room.

Nell was there, setting the table, the baby quiet on a blanket spread on the floor and the boy busy with blocks in the corner. The boy spotted Reese and climbed to his small feet, and Reese crossed to him, lifting him in the air, holding him above his head.

The boy shrieked with pleasure and Reese laughed at him. Jenny watched, touched at the humanness which had survived in Reese despite everything. The old gentleness she had known was still there beneath the toughened exterior.

Unconsciously she glanced at Creed, who

showed no interest in the children. True, they were the children of his old enemy but she felt that he would have ignored any youngsters.

And suddenly she wondered, was this what she missed in Creed's makeup? With all his studied kindnesses to her and even to Reese, she could not recall a single act of instinctive gentleness made by Creed.

All during dinner she watched the two men, surprised and vaguely uneasy at Creed's talkativeness; he who was usually so silent in the presence of others.

"Duke's got to try to move those cattle," he was telling Carstairs. "Put yourself in his shoes. He stopped your man from going to Texas, but by now he'll know you've sent another. Wouldn't you try to cash in before those records got here?"

Reese nodded and Creed went on, like a general outlining a campaign.

"If it were me, I'd get an injunction from the judge, a court order forbidding Duke to move those cows until your proof of ownership arrives. After all, the will has not yet been probated and the court certainly has the right to prevent any removal of property involved."

Joe Blunt had been eating diligently and listening. He looked up from the far end of the table, pointing his knife at Reese.

"Captain, that sounds like a good idea."

Reese glanced from one to the other, his tone noncommittal. "I'll hunt up the judge after dinner."

"You won't have to hunt far." Creed laughed. "You can be certain to find him at the poker game. It's a wonder he doesn't hold his court there between hands."

Creed said no more on the subject, and when the dinner was finished he stayed to smoke a cigar as Reese pushed back his plate and rose.

Joe Blunt got up like Carstairs' shadow. He had not allowed his captain out of the building alone and now he stepped into the twilight of the porch beside Reese.

He lighted his short-stemmed pipe, using the time to study the quiet street before he nodded and fell into step as Reese started for the saloon.

"That Creed seems like a good one to ride with. It's hard to figure after the way he was shooting up the Triple X when we came in."

Reese did not answer and Blunt went on. "Glad he thought of the injunction."

"I guess so." Reese sounded thoughtful.

The ex-sergeant looked at him, knowing him as well as one man can know another. They had shared the command of the Raiders for so long now that Blunt could nearly guess an order before Reese gave it.

"What's troubling you, Captain?"

With Whitey he could have argued out his

doubts and though Blunt was not so quick to comprehend, still Reese felt the need to put into words the vague feelings that disturbed him.

"Several things," he said, "don't seem to add up. Mostly, it's somehow out of character for Creed to be so all fired anxious to help me. Look at it from his angle. He's been fighting Alf and Duke over grass for years. Why isn't he fighting me? And supposing Duke got away with the cattle, cleared the range, wouldn't you think that would be the natural thing for Creed to want?"

Joe Blunt pushed back his battered hat and scratched his grizzled head.

"It don't make much sense, does it, Captain? Unless he just likes you, figures if he helps you get Duke, you might be a friendly neighbor for a change."

"He could afford to wait and see about that. Does he strike you as a man who just likes people?"

Blunt turned it over in his mind for half a block and shook his head slowly. "Beats me. What do you intend to do?"

"Watch, and try to figure out what his game is."

They went on in silence, each working at the puzzle, and turned in at the saloon, Joe Blunt walking past the bar with real regret that he had no money. He had always been a drinking man and it had been a long time since he had tasted anything but the hot raw tequila and mescal liquor they had occasionally been given by the Mexican Indians.

They found the judge in his accustomed chair, Hawthorne on his left and four others around the table waiting for the deal as one shuffled the worn cards. Alf looked up as Reese paused beside them, and Hawthorne asked, "How's Whitey?"

"Seems to be holding his own," Carstairs said, and asked for the injunction.

Judge Burke sat back, rocking the front feet of his chair up from the floor, leaning against the wall and sighing.

"You've got the right. What I wonder is, will it do any good? Duke's not likely to be much impressed by the law unless it favors him. Matter of fact an injunction might make him move a little faster."

Reese said levelly, "It would do one thing. Hawthorne could swear us in as special deputies if he does start to drive the herd. We'd have the law with us to stop him."

Burke shrugged heavily. He tipped forward and rose.

"So be it. Come on over to the courthouse. You too, Hawthorne, you'll have to serve Borden. And I don't envy you the job."

It was plain on Hawthorne's old face that he agreed with the judge, but he rose obediently, and together they returned to the street.

THIRTEEN

Duke Borden stood alone in the Triple X yard staring up the lush valley where small brown dots marked the leisurely grazing animals of the Carstairs herd. The early morning sun heightened the colors of the land and warmed the night's chill from his big frame, but neither its pleasant heat nor the peace of the scene could shake the man from the brooding uneasiness that held him.

He had come so far, and now he had blundered, and from here on it would be hard. Borden did not mind a fight, if it came to that, but his slow patience was burning out and he felt an urge to beat his huge fists on the heads of those who still thwarted him.

Behind him he heard noise, and turned to see the sheriff, Hawthorne, ride deliberately up the lane and into the yard and pause to wait the customary courtesy of the land.

Borden nodded, wariness in his eyes, his mind working at the reason which had called for this visit.

"Light down," he said. "Take the weight off

your behind." Even Hawthorne had hesitated to approach this ranch in the darkness unannounced and he glanced now around the quiet yard, seeing no one but Borden and wondering at the whereabouts of the crew before he stepped from the saddle. Methodically he came toward Borden, a deceptive ease in his manner, reaching into his pocket and drawing out a paper and handing it forward.

"An official visit, Duke," he said, and put the paper into Borden's palm.

"Official?" Duke stood stolid, his boot heels together, his head inches above that of the old sheriff. Slowly he unfolded the paper and began to read, and as his mind grasped the sense of the words angry color spread up beneath his deep tan. He finished his reading, his lips following the letters, and then raised his head to look boldly into the sheriff's steady gaze.

As their eyes held, Duke Borden's hands folded the paper, tore it into pieces and opened, letting the slips flutter to the ground at his feet.

He could not find a smile to match his arrogant words.

"To hell with it."

Hawthorne sighed, shaking his head.

"You're a fool, Duke. That paper is a court order. If you violate it we'll have a clear case against you. We'll bring you in if I have to deputize every man in the Park to do it."

Frustration goaded Borden's temper. "Get on your horse," he said, tightness making his voice rasp. "Get off this ranch. And anybody you send out here had better be wearing something besides a tin star."

His breathing was hard as he watched Hawthorne nod stiffly, remount and without excitement turn his horse out of the yard. Then Borden spun on his heel and stormed into the house.

Standing beside the desk that had been Alf Carstairs', Duke found himself trembling, and that fact further infuriated him, rage roiling in him as in a tormented bull.

The corroding envy of the Carstairs family which had dominated his entire life had grown inevitably into personal hatred and a determination to take possession of all they held.

Years ago Reese's love for Nell had given Duke his first glimpse of opportunity, and he had fostered their hoped for union, in his young mind building a farsighted plan with such care that not even his own family had been aware of the extent of his dream.

Circumstances had changed but still favored him and he had used them well. Now, with his goal almost in his grasp he had lost his head twice. Frightening Nell and the children away while Reese was still around had been the first mistake and he had panicked when Whitey started for Texas. The attempt to kill the rider had been pointless, he saw that now, and worse, it had served to harden Reese's resolve against him. The injunction was proof of that.

And tearing up the paper, threatening Hawthorne was indeed the act of a fool. He shook his head groggily as if to clear it. There must be no more mistakes.

He had a grudging respect for Hawthorne. For all his plodding ways, his quiet casualness, the sheriff never backed off from a job.

Reese himself was formidable enough, and with the law at his back he was twice as dangerous. His own next move, already planned, would require more than his usual care.

He had, he felt, one real advantage. He was expected to attempt a cattle drive and this he had no intention of doing.

In his present mood even this thought failed to please him.

He crossed to the table and poured himself half a glass of whiskey, his mouth turning down sourly as he saw the shaking of the hand that held the glass. He dumped the liquor in a burning draught down his big throat, then went to the door and shouted for Mart January.

The rider came at a half-run from the bunkhouse.

"Get into town and find out what's going on," Duke told him, managing now to control his voice, to conceal the emotions within him. "Don't make trouble. I want to know if Carstairs is still at the hotel, and where his men are."

Without words January nodded and moved away. It was well past dark when he returned to the Triple X. Wearily he dismounted and left his horse at the corral, then turned toward the main house where lamplight still brightened the wide windows.

His boss sat heavily at the table in the front room, the whiskey bottle at his elbow, now nearly empty. Yet he knew that Borden was not drunk. Borden would have apportioned whatever the bottle had held with the same studied care he put into everything he did. As long as January had known him, he had not seen Borden drunk.

He helped himself to a drink as Duke indicated the bottle, and waited for Duke's question.

"What did you find out?"

"Carstairs is still at the hotel. He has one man with him and it looks like Hawthorne and his two deputies are keeping an eye on him, like they figure we might try something. The one they call Pop Greer is on his way to Texas and the Raiders rode with him to Denver. They're not back yet."

Duke Borden considered, nodding. He leaned back in the chair and stretched hugely, and smiled for the first time that day.

"About the way I figured it. When they get back Carstairs will take them out to the camp again. We'll hit them then. We've got to be ready. I want no slipup. We clear them out and stop Greer coming in from Texas. Without the proof he's bringing, Alf's will is good as gold."

He shoved back the chair and rose, noting the single remaining shot of whiskey and raised the bottle to his thick lips, draining it.

Mart January was grinning, understanding the full scope of Duke's plan and admiring it. He waved good night and left the house as Borden reached up to extinguish the hanging lamp.

The week that followed was busy for Borden, organizing his attack, spending most of his time exploring the canyon camp, studying how best to spring his trap.

A thousand yards above the campsite he found a side draw down which a man could ride, but the spot Reese and Joe Blunt had purposely chosen was protected by sharply rising walls. The camp hugged the north side of the canyon where the stream had gouged out a narrow cut in the solid rock face, creating an overhang.

Along this opening Joe Blunt had built a barricade of logs, V-shaped, protected from above by the overhang and covering both the up and down approaches to the camp.

Borden and January rode unmolested

through this now deserted fortlike construction, and at last Borden grunted in satisfaction.

"Send Keller over to the North Star mine," he said. "Have him get us some powder and fuse."

Mart January had been wondering how his boss intended to attack a group so well prepared, and a smile twisted his narrow lips now as he turned away.

They mined the log buttress next day, and ran the long fuse through the sandy soil bordering the creek, then up the steep bank to a point where a man could creep unseen to light it at the proper time.

Duke assigned places to each of his men and rehearsed them painstakingly, making his instructions minutely inclusive. His timing was lucky, for early the second night the Raiders returned from Denver.

For the first time since Whitey's injury Joe Blunt left Reese Carstairs' side, delegating Bo Martin to the watch, and led Austin and Gil Martin back to the canyon camp.

Duke had been careful, but Blunt's searching eyes read the sign of men and horses around the barricade, and he rode farther up the canyon, coming back grim-faced.

"Our visitors went to some trouble to cover their tracks." He stepped down and stood, his short legs wide apart, his head thrown back as he scanned the brush above them.

"I don't like it," he decided. "I'm going back and tell the captain we'd best move. You two boys get the gear together. I won't be long."

He rode out fast, unaware that Borden's man had been watching from his post high on the mountain, and at first sight of their return, had streaked for the Triple X.

Joe Blunt reached town without trouble, stalking into the hotel lobby where Reese sat with Nell and the children. Reese came at once to his feet.

"What's happened?"

Joe shook his gray head. "Nothing yet. And maybe I'm being spooked, but there's been somebody nosing around the camp. It's a good place, water and lots of grass, but I smell a trap."

"Then we move."

Joe grunted. "I just wanted to know where to. The boys are getting ready."

Nell cut in, saying, "Ben Creed told Reese you were welcome at his place any time you wanted to come."

Joe Blunt looked at Reese. "Creed still here?"

"He and Jenny went for a walk." It was Nell again. Reese was silent, hesitating.

It was a long way from town to Creed's place, and he could not yet move Whitey. Also, he intended to meet Pop Greer again in Denver on his return, but the round trip to

Texas would take at least a couple of weeks and something had to be done about the men now.

Nell seemed to be thinking the same and said, "The sensible thing would be to bring them to the hotel again. You should all be together while you're fighting Duke."

Reese nodded, suddenly finding that he could be amused at this girl's generosity when it might expedite something she wanted.

"All right," he said. "But when Creed comes back tell him we may be taking advantage of his offer soon. I'll ride out for the boys with Blunt. We'll be a couple of hours."

He climbed the stairs at a lope, glad to be moving again, feeling the strain that waiting in idleness had put upon him.

Whitey Ellis' face was bleached and drawn, but he was awake and his blue lips twisted in a tiny smile. It was about the only movement he had the strength for.

Bo Martin hunched in the chair beside the bed, but he spun as Reese came in and his sharp, sensitive face tightened, noting the change in his captain.

Carstairs wasted no words. "I'll be gone two hours or so with Joe. Don't leave the hotel until we get back. We're moving camp, maybe out to Creed's."

The Cajun nodded, saying nothing, and Reese walked to the bed to lay a light hand on Ellis' bony shoulder. They looked at each other for a long moment of understanding before Reese turned out of the room.

It was full dark when they left town, the high arch of the night sky luminous with the promise of moonlight, and the meadow around them spread with a light mist that rose from the streams and hid the lower swales, giving Reese the eerie feeling that he rode on islands through a quiet sea. Joe Blunt's voice came to him in a low growl, betraying the deep resentment of a weary man who has sought peace for years and failed to find it.

"Why wait for Pop to get back?" he said. "Why don't we hit Duke now? For my part I've taken all the pushing and crowding I care for."

Reese considered the words honestly, wondering at his own reluctance. His determination to stop Duke, to get back his own was as strong as ever. But Jenny's plea had crystallized his desire to gain the victory lawfully — without arms. He had seen a mockery made of the law in other lands and the suffering caused by it. And the last week had erased the urge for personal vengeance.

His feeling for the girl had grown stronger than his hatred of Duke Borden, stronger than anything he had ever experienced. Being near her, becoming aware of serenity, appreciating her quick response to the moods of others, he had surrendered to the need of her gentle steadiness.

Any fear that his affection for her might be only a turning away from the lonely disillusionment with Nell was gone.

He knew that his love for Nell would never have kept him from his set course, and that his feeling for Jenny would hold for as long as he lived.

He could not say these things to Joe Blunt, and explained instead, "When we have the law behind us we will move. I'm not spending the rest of my life on the dodge, even to settle the score with Duke. I've wasted enough years as it is."

Blunt sighed, discontented, but following his captain, and they rode on toward the hills rising darkly, outlined now by the coming moon.

Without foreknowledge they rode directly into Borden's men, and the Triple X crew was as surprised as they. Duke's riders had swept across the lower hills to take up their prearranged positions in the canyon mouth.

Through the timber-shadowed darkness Duke heard the horses on the trail, and with his men scattered, thought his orders were not being followed. Cursing, warning them in a heavy whisper to wait his signal to attack, he stepped from his hiding place almost at Carstairs' stirrup.

Reese heard the voice and at once envisioned the trap and wheeled as his horse ran past the gesturing Borden. His rifle was in its boot beneath his leg. He pulled his Colts and fired toward Duke, but his horse spooked at the instant and the shots went wild.

Bullets reached for him from the brush and Reese heard Borden's high wild yell as he leaped back behind his rocks.

At his flank Joe Blunt was shouting. "Get out of here, Captain. Ride."

He slapped the rump of Reese's horse with the barrel of his short gun and spurred his own animal, and the two drove forward, touching each other, Borden's riders firing after them until they rounded a bend in the canyon's twisting way and ran their horses up the sloping trail toward the camp.

Ahead of them, Austin had been cooking dinner over the small fire while Gil Martin led the horses from the corral toward the stream. The first shots in the canyon's mouth brought them around to rush toward the barricade where their guns were stacked, then to crouch concealed, covering the downward trail.

They heard the pound of horses coming up, and only held their fire in time at Reese's warning shout.

"It's Borden. Hit the brush."

Reese threw himself from his saddle and lit running, heading for the barricade and the extra ammunition cached there. He did not reach it.

Borden's powder man, scrabbling for his post, had reached it, lost his head and lighted the fuse. The explosive beneath the logs blew, tossing the barricade into the air and scattering a wave of sand which nearly blinded Carstairs. Martin staggered and fell, his piercing scream echoing in the narrow defile.

Across the canyon another of Borden's guns opened fire and Joe Blunt was off his horse, snatching his rifle from its boot as Reese dived for Martin. He caught up the small figure in his arms and dashed on, bent over, making for the shelter of the dark trees beyond the radius of Austin's firelight.

Reese saw Joe Blunt grab Austin, propel the still blast-shocked Raider forward. And then they were beside him, Joe Blunt helping to drag the wounded man up the sharp bank, so steep here that they must haul themselves by grasping tree limbs.

The ground was deep soft with leaf mold, and they moved with the silence of long practice, hearing behind them the occasional telltale sounds of Borden's hunt for them. Joe Blunt took the lead, his gun drawn, alert for sounds ahead. Reese still carrying Martin and Austin, his head cleared now, following as rear guard.

The moon had not yet touched this side of the mountain and they worked higher in the deep shadow, not stopping until they neared the rim where a level spot stretched between two rock outbursts, and here Reese collapsed to his knees, easing his burden to the ground.

For a while he fought for breath and as his gasping slowed he tried to listen. Around them was a heavy stillness, even the ordinary night noises of animals strangely missing and the eerie sense touched Reese that Borden's crew could hear him breathe.

He stayed on his knees beside Gil Martin, and now with his hands made a careful examination. He found the wound in the man's neck, the great mass of sticky wetness spreading from it, dripping onto his own hands.

Martin had lost much blood. Reese found it on his coat, on his shirt, and guessed that it was splashed across the rocks in the path of their passage to mark their trail.

Far below he saw a lantern bob and swore softly to himself. He set himself to lift the wounded man again, and sensed the difference in the heft of Martin's weight before he paused to feel for a pulse.

The Cajun's wrist was still. Reese straightened slowly, cursing Borden anew, and found the shape of Joe Blunt's shadow close ahead. Austin he could not see, but he called softly, "Gil's gone."

He heard a low oath from each and said, "Let's get out of here." He reached for Martin's gun and had to pry it from the fingers frozen around it. His back was turned when Blunt raised his rifle and fired at the bobbing lantern. He heard the thin scream and saw the lantern fall and swore at Blunt.

It was one of the few times in a dozen years that the man had lost his head. He didn't blame him now, but the shot had given away their position.

His own urge was to charge down the mountainside, to confront Duke Borden and finish it between them, but the habit of command was strong, and he still had men alive to get safely out of this trap.

Sharply he called to them and started ahead, crawling along the canyon side, not looking back but hearing that they followed.

Below them the firing had ceased and he judged that Borden's men were fanning out, scaling the canyon wall toward them.

The gun above kept up a measured, steady fire, the sniper spreading his shots across the brush in the hope of a lucky hit. Then a warning voice yelled from below.

"Hold it, you fool. You'll hit one of us. Just make sure they don't go over the rim."

Austin laughed softly, his shoulder touching Reese as they crawled together. Austin could always laugh when the going was tight. He said in a whispered undertone,

"We're sandwiched. Where to, Captain?"

"Down the hill. They won't expect that,

and there are horses that way if we can reach them. If we came out on top we'd be afoot. They'd hunt us down by daylight."

They turned downward again, their bodies touching, angling toward the canyon's mouth, taking their time, making no noise and constantly listening for sign of Borden's crew.

They were halfway down the face, at the brink of a drop so sharp that only the trees prevented their falling into the stream below. It was entirely dark here. The distant moon that had at last topped the ridge was screened from them by the timber.

Then a muffled curse was flung unwittingly from a man who stumbled and fell heavily on their right, and Duke Borden's voice carried out of the darkness.

"Careful."

Reese froze and felt Blunt and Austin stiffen. They stayed where they were, motionless as the mountain against which they crouched, hardly daring to breathe, their guns held ready.

If they were discovered here they had no chance of retreat, and Reese felt certain that Borden's men were on either side of them.

They lay listening, hearing the scrambling as the unseen man regained his feet and started on up the mountain. Reese could not be sure if Borden moved with him or was holding his place, and they continued to wait as minutes dragged out like so many trying years.

Yet they had to move soon, before the moon should reach a height where its light would flood the canyon and betray them all. Reese reached out, touching Blunt and Austin and then began his careful descent, thankful for the soft soil, grateful that there were no loose rocks to be dislodged and racket into the depths.

He found a pole pine, its five-inch trunk thrust straight toward the sky and made sure of his grip. Then, seated, he slid downward until his feet rested against a lower tree. Again and again he repeated the slide and was surprised when the bank abruptly leveled out and he stood beside the rushing stream. He could hear nothing against its roar and stood tense, waiting until Austin and Blunt were at his shoulder.

There was no way of knowing how many waited for them at the bottom of the canyon, for certainly Borden would not have left that exit unguarded, but there was no choice. They had to try for the horses.

Reese had no watch, but the smell of morning was already in the air and he guessed that the sky would begin to lighten within the hour.

Again he touched the other two and they turned down the stream. Reese held his gun and Martin's, blinking and staring, trying to pierce the darkness, to spot any movement before him.

He heard the horses, then smelled them, long before their shapes loomed out of the still trees, and his heart quickened. If they could make it to the animals. If there were not too many guards.

He crept forward, Blunt and Austin at his flanks, moving like shadows. He reached out to take the bridle of the nearest horse, and suddenly a man was standing within five feet of him.

Even as he caught his breath the guard's gun flashed out, almost in his face.

It was Joe Blunt who saved his life, leaping from the darkness to crash the heavy barrel of his gun across the guard's head, felling the man who landed on his face and remained motionless.

The horses had been picketed to trees. They spooked now from nervousness, but Austin had one freed, then a second and Reese loosened a third. Apparently there was not another guard for no one halted their retreat. Above them guns were hammering from the canyon side, but they rounded the curve without being hit and spurred toward the town whose lights now showed faintly in the far distance.

FOURTEEN

Duke Borden led his sullen crew home to the Triple X. It was still not daylight and like ghosts they trailed through the lowland fog, appearing and disappearing among the damp white clouds. The dirt that coated their faces from the night's work caught the moisture and streaked, until each looked as if he wore an Indian's war paint.

Borden's soundless rage was ominous. But for the mischance that Reese Carstairs and Joe Blunt had surprised him, he felt certain that he could have wiped out the lot. He had failed again and he was too vain a man ever to accept failure with any grace.

The crew kept out of his way as they reached the ranch, thronging unwashed into the cookshack for a tense breakfast and then slipping toward the bunkhouse.

Borden let them sleep until midday, himself falling fully dressed across Alf's bed but failing to find rest. At noon he cursed them up, ordering January to saddle his horse and followed the foreman to the corral.

There was only one course left open for him now and there in the open privacy he gave the order.

"Start rounding up the herd," he said, and swore again at January's uncertain glance.

"What happens," said the rider, "when you start the drive? With that court order, Hawthorne is bound to make a play."

Duke spat at the ground. "We'll get them through." Still January hesitated, but he was less afraid of Borden, knowing what his boss was planning.

"Duke," he insisted, "listen. I've stood by you all the way. And I'm not forgetting that you promised me a tenth share in the ranch if I killed Carstairs."

"If you killed them both. If you hadn't botched it we wouldn't be in this jackpot now. You'll still get your tenth of what the herd brings at the railroad."

January grunted, knowing less a loyalty to Borden than a dogged hunger for the things Borden had held out to him. It was not likely that anywhere else he could come into possession of the value of one tenth of this herd.

"I'll go along," he said grudgingly, "because I haven't much choice. But how sure are you of the crew? A couple of them are already backing off, saying you were too rough on your sister."

Borden shrugged his irritation. "Get rid of those, now. For the rest, they'd all cut your throat for a hundred silver dollars. Offer them that as a bonus, a hundred to every man with us when the cattle are sold."

Still January was not satisfied. Duke's recent failures were nagging his mind.

"The odds are against you, Duke, and you know it. The sheriff can deputize half the men in the Park."

Borden's surliness broke suddenly in derisive laughter.

"Deputize who? Get next to yourself. Who's going to serve? Would you fight the Triple X to save those cows for Reese Carstairs?"

"No."

"Can you name anyone that would? Think about it. There's not an outfit or a man in the Park not afraid of us. They may hate our guts, but they damn well think too much of their own hides to risk catching one of our bullets."

January stubbornly held his ground. "Creed would. You've pushed him hard and he's tough and strong. His crew's nearly as big as ours."

"I'll take care of Creed."

"How?"

Borden cursed the man aloud, hating to explain himself but needing January beside him at this time.

"Use your head for something except to hold up your hat. Who, after me, stands to profit most if I get the cattle away? Creed, doesn't he? If Carstairs keeps them here he and Creed will be at each other's throats over range within a week.

"Creed's no fool. He'll be on my side. He'll help us move the herd. He ought to pay me for leaving."

January was surprised. "You've talked to him?"

"I'm going to. Now. At his ranch."

He mounted the horse and looked down at his lieutenant, feeling the man's doubt and the need to encourage him.

"You just get the roundup started. We won't try to go over the pass. They could block that. We'll drive west toward Encampment and then cut north. We'll have more room that way."

He swung the horse before January could answer, and spurred toward Creed's. The ride took nearly an hour, but he turned into the long lane unhurried, letting the animal pick its own gait.

Clem Davis saw him coming a good quarter of a mile from the house. Two of the crew were at the blacksmith shop repairing a broken wagon reach and Davis called to them, and so had a reception committee of three to face Borden in the trampled yard.

He made no movement to dismount under the neutral stares, but indicated his peaceful intentions by crossing his hands on the high pommel of his saddle and even finding a smile of sorts.

"Creed around?"

"In town."

Davis' voice was expressionless, his eyes watchful, his mind wondering what possible business would bring Duke Borden calling here.

Borden hesitated, not expecting this and uncertain whether Davis was lying. Yet there was no sign of life from the main house, and after a moment he reined his horse around with a muttered word and loped back the way he had come.

The beauty of the land, the pleasantness of the weather were lost on him, and he spent the ride in a favorite occupation, day-dreaming of what he would do when he attained the Carstairs' stature. Reese had no claim on the Triple X itself but Duke realized that once he violated the court injunction by driving the cattle he could hardly expect to come back unmolested by the law. Still the herd was the most valuable asset of the Triple X and once he had the money from its sale, he could find another ranch, register a new brand and build bigger than ever.

He was in a better humor when at dusk he rode up before the saloon at Walden and stepped down to enter the long, already lamplighted room. He wanted no meeting with Carstairs at this time, and went quietly to the bar, stopping beside two of the townsmen there. He smiled, and spoke in a voice low enough that it would not carry to the poker table beyond,

"Either of you know where Ben Creed is?"

The tall man at the right was startled, but he chose not to offend Duke Borden.

"He was here until a few minutes ago. He went up to the hotel for supper."

"Want to make a dollar?"

The man was not sure that he did, but Borden drew a silver coin from his pocket and said easily,

"Tell Creed I want to see him at the livery. It's peaceful." He grinned then, and the man shrugged, accepting the mission.

Borden watched him go, had a slow drink, then went out to his horse and rode leisurely up the street to the barn. He was seated in one of the chairs beside the wide doorway when Creed came deliberately along the sidewalk, his eyes watchful as if he expected a trap.

Borden was amused to see him wary, proud that he had the power to make this man whom he hated show caution. With intentional rudeness he made no effort to rise, leaning back, keeping his hands folded in his lap. He grinned viciously as Creed paused before him to stare downward.

"What are you afraid of, Ben?"

"Snakes," said Creed. "People who strike when your back's turned. What's on your mind, Duke?"

Borden's grin widened. "Just thought you'd like to know that I'm moving out. Your man up in the timber must be tired of watching for me to round up the beef. I thought I'd save him the trouble of reporting."

"Thanks. Is that all?"

"I'm here to offer a deal."

"Why should I deal with you?"

"For the only reason you do anything, a favor to yourself. I'm taking the cattle to Wyoming."

"Against the court order?"

Borden used a thick thumb to shove his hat farther back on his big head.

"The court order. It has no value across the state line."

"It has value here." Creed sounded as if the man's arrogance amused him. "Hawthorne means business, Duke. He was at the hotel today, talking to Carstairs."

"Let him talk," Borden scoffed. "What'll he use for manpower? Carstairs has two men available, Hawthorne has two deputies. You think any noble citizen is going to volunteer against us and get his head shot off?"

"I might."

Duke Borden was genuine startled. Then he took the words as a jest.

"Very funny. But I know you're smarter

than that. The best thing that can happen to you is my taking those cows out and leaving you the range you've been bellyaching for."

"True." Creed continued to smile faintly.

Borden's eyes showed his puzzlement. "Then what are you trying to do?"

"Men don't always act in accordance with their best interests. Sometimes they deliberately go against them."

"That's stupid. Why should you help Carstairs?"

Creed shook his head in mock sympathy. "You're the one who's stupid, Duke. You wouldn't understand me. You're a money-grubbing hog. You never had anything except a certain animal cunning, and now you're losing that."

He turned on his heel and sauntered back toward the hotel, leaving Borden open-mouthed behind him. But he worked with a growing elation which he had to control. Things were working almost exactly as he had foreseen, and ahead of him lay the chance he had been awaiting to turn the coming events to his own complete advantage.

He felt a lightness, a buoyancy, but he held his steps to a measured tread, mounting the porch and coming into the empty lobby. Voices from the kitchen attracted him and he went that way, finding Nell at the scrubbed table giving the baby its evening bath while Reese helped Jenny with the dishes. Nell looked up, then haughtily withdrew her eyes.

Jenny turned around, her smile of welcome warming him.

"I put your supper in the oven, Ben. What did Duke want?"

Ben Creed would have liked to take her into his arms, to kiss her thoroughly, and he put this into his answering smile before he moved to the oven for his food, got a knife and fork and sat down in one of the kitchen chairs, balancing his plate on his knee. He held his words until he was settled, hoping that Carstairs would turn to him. Reese did not, and Creed finally said, "He's moving the herd out. He wanted to be sure I didn't interfere."

Jenny caught her breath and Carstairs said, "What did you tell him?" His back was still to Creed as he finished the last of the dishes.

"I didn't promise." Creed's tone had gained a tiny mocking edge. "His point was that taking the cattle would be to my advantage, would give me back my grass."

"It would do that." Reese Carstairs picked up the hand towel and methodically dried his hands before facing around. "From your viewpoint it should be a perfect deal."

Creed did not answer, and covered the silence by taking a forkful of food into his mouth. Carstairs walked across to stand over him.

"I've been wondering about that angle ever since your offer of help. What about it? What are you thinking?"

"Reese." Jenny sounded disapproving. "That's hardly a nice thing to say to Ben."

He spoke without looking at her. "I'm no longer a very nice person, Jenny. Any niceness I had has been squeezed out of me. I try to play it fair, but I'm also a realist. People and things are as they are. I expect no miracles and I don't expect unselfish generosity from Ben Creed."

Creed chuckled. "You're so right."

He ignored the two women, the baby who had begun to whimper, and the watching boy. He rose easily, leaning across to set his empty plate on the drainboard. Then he straightened in front of Reese and said in an even, unmoved voice, "I'll say to you what I said to Duke Borden. Men do not always do what appears to be best for them. Sometimes there are reasons to make them act quite to the contrary. I'll tell you what I did not tell Borden, that in my case the opinion of a third party is more important to me than all the grass in the world."

He glanced at Jenny and in satisfaction saw the color rise richly to her face. Then he pivoted with military precision and marched out of the kitchen.

He left a long, unbroken silence behind him until finally Jenny turned back to the sink and picked up Creed's dish to wash. Nell watched after the departed Creed with deep speculation, then faced her sister.

"I think," she said, "you had better quit being so cavalier with him. A chance like that does not come to a girl like you every day."

Jenny's head went up, but she said nothing. Neither was conscious of Reese at the moment. He stood rock-still, watching the two of them, and told himself that Nell was right, though her reasoning was wrong. Creed had everything to offer the younger girl while he, Reese, was at this reckoning on the land, his only possession a horse and its gear, and a hard fight ahead before he could realistically ask her to share his life.

Creed was smart. With all the material things he could offer Jenny he asked instead that she judge him on his treatment of his rival. Apparently he was also a gambler. When Duke started the drive and they rode against him, men would die. Creed's chances of survival were better than his own by a slight edge. Reese's death was of more importance to Duke.

Without speaking he got his coat from the chair back, thrust into it and walked with purpose toward the lobby. He reached the stairs and mounted them, going to his room. From the bureau drawer he lifted his gun belt and fastened it around his waist. As he settled it, noise from the hall brought him around to see Jenny stop in the open doorway, her eyes wide on the belt.

He knew she had misunderstood, thought he was taking a lone hand for a showdown with Duke. She opened her mouth to speak and then did not. Instead she stepped back into the hall.

"Jenny."

She did not stop.

"Jenny, listen to me."

"There's nothing to say." She stopped then, but without looking up.

"I'll try to talk to him, to make him see reason. But I can't go unarmed."

She raised her face to him then, her dark eyes almost black, and her head moved from side to side.

"You know him better than that."

"I've got to try. If he moves the cattle, men will be killed, Hawthorne and his deputies, Creed and his crew. It's my fight, not theirs. Do you want me to risk all of them?"

She did not answer. Her drawn face watched him a moment longer, then she moved on down the hall, her young shoulders sagging with a hopelessness she could not conceal.

He watched her go, his own hopelessness matching hers, then he picked up the heavy gun, checked it, shoved it into his holster and walked softly toward the stairs.

Purposely he did not take the Raiders. His only chance of swaying Borden would be in privacy, where Duke would not seem to be backing down on a taken course.

Outside it was dark and the yellow glow of the lantern within the livery window showed him Borden still in the cane-bottomed chair, tipped back against the wall. He did not at first see Hawthorne, standing beyond the lantern's path, and walked slowly forward.

Duke glanced up. Duke saw him corning, and his lips twisted and he spoke to the sheriff. Reese saw the older man then, too late to turn back, and knew at once that Hawthorne had misunderstood.

He watched the sheriff stiffen his shoulders against the wall and watched his hands move slowly down to hang near the holstered gun, and heard him call across the dozen feet that separated them,

"Go back to the hotel, Captain. Put that gun away."

Reese shook his head. "I want to talk to Duke, Sheriff, alone. I'm still trying to live by the rules."

Hawthorne nodded. "See that you do. I've just warned Duke that if he moves the cattle he'll have every man I can raise against him."

He did not leave and Carstairs said again, "Let me talk to him."

Borden's laughter cut across the words. "Talk about what, Captain, the army of storekeepers who'll try to stop me? Do you really think they'll ride against the Triple X?"

"I'll ride against you, and Creed with me.

We're too many for you, Duke. You can't drive cows and fight at the same time. I'm keeping those cattle here if I have to kill your whole crew."

Again Borden laughed, goading Reese. "Why don't you start now, Captain? Why don't you shoot me here?"

Reese Carstairs clenched his teeth together, trying to keep back the words, but Duke Borden had pushed too far.

"Stand up, Duke," he said. "Reach for your gun."

Wickedly Borden looked up at Hawthorne, his grin a gloating thing.

"There's your hero, Sheriff. With a gun in his belt he's ready to challenge an unarmed man."

He raised his arms to show his lap. Purposely he had not worn his weapon in trying to bargain with Creed. He had felt much safer without it.

Reese stared at him, then wiped his hand across his eyes and with a murmured word turned blindly away.

FIFTEEN

There were two possible routes northward to the railroad camps. One along the Platte, past the old Indian Encampment, the other a twisting trail which followed Pinkham Creek to where it came out of Kings Canyon into the central valley.

The Kings Canyon trail was narrow, rocky, winding, strewn with huge boulders, steeply walled a thousand feet above the rushing creek. At the upper end where it flattened into deep meadows and tiny mountain parks, beavers had built a hundred dams, flooding the hollows into shallow lakes, some extending over fifty acres.

Here there were dangerous bog holes which could mire an animal belly-deep and no man in his right mind would send cattle in any numbers through such a natural trap.

Still both routes must be covered as they had no way of guessing which Borden would choose. He was proceeding as if he expected no interference and the first real intimation of his strategy came with the appearance of strange riders drifting through Walden, asking for the Triple X.

No one knew exactly how many there were, but they kept coming, by twos, by threes, hard-eyed, taciturn men who volunteered nothing, moving like sinister shadows forerunning impending storm.

Hawthorne watched them, his mouth beneath the straggly line of mustache seeming to grow thinner by the hour.

The valley watched. No community likes warfare and most of the people in the Park had seen range wars even if they had not been actively engaged.

The running battle which Alf Carstairs had carried on with Ben Creed had been confined, not affecting the majority of inhabitants directly. But they knew Hawthorne would take action against Duke Borden with the movement of the first Triple X stock from the home range.

He had called for volunteers, and men who had been his close associates for years avoided him on the street and one of his deputies quit. Only two came forth to be deputized, Moose Kobbler and Pete Mullins.

The sheriff had been taken aback by the appearance of these two. Kobbler, still wearing the wristlets that were the mark of his trade, his voice betraying self-consciousness, had explained:

"I figure a storekeeper better back up the

law if he aims to stay in business. I ain't much of a hand with a gun, Sheriff, but I been practicin'."

Hawthorne nodded and looked at the cook from the Triple X. The only sign of emotion in Pete's voice was a slight thickening of his natural brogue.

"I worked for Alf Carstairs a long while," he said.

The lawman accepted both of them and knew there would be no others.

He was with Judge Burke in the old courtroom when Reese came to the door. He turned around, nodding a greeting and waited as Carstairs walked forward to the bench.

"I wouldn't have believed it, Reese." Hawthorne sounded tired. "Only two have agreed to serve — a storekeeper and a cook." He spread his hands helplessly. "If it wouldn't look as if I were avoiding a fight I'd take off the badge and resign. A law officer whose community won't support him is valueless."

Judge Burke ran a hand through his thick hair, watching Reese intently.

Reese said, "This is my fight. Maybe I shouldn't have asked for the injunction. When Creed suggested it, I thought it was a good idea."

Both the judge and Hawthorne looked surprised.

"Creed? Why would he take an interest in your problem?"

Reese did not change expression. He saw no reason to bring Jenny's name into it. He shrugged. "He has his reasons. He's offered to help."

Hawthorne was blunt. "Do you trust him?"

"Not entirely."

The three men looked at one another consideringly. It was Burke who broke the silence.

"It's a bad thing when law and order breaks down. I've seen it happen in half a dozen places. I hate to see it here. If Duke's allowed to flaunt the court, others will follow." He spoke directly to Reese. "I'm not taking your side. Until you prove you own the cattle, I have no opinion. But I won't stand by and let Duke Borden ignore a court order. There's far more at stake here than this single case."

Carstairs appraised Burke, seeing him in a new light. Before he had thought that Burke's casual attitude was the outward indication of a tired cynicism. In this moment he realized there was a dignity of purpose, a deep belief in the sanctity of the law in the judge.

It was such as this man educated, trained, dedicated, who had brought a surprising amount of control to the frontiers of the country and Reese felt shame that he had been about to suggest the court order be withdrawn, leaving the fight between Duke Borden and himself.

Burke might have been reading his mind. "We can't back down," he said. "Sheriff, you can swear me in as a special deputy. I've already written to the governor. In actuality there is not much he can do. We have no militia and I doubt if he would declare martial law in a case like this."

Hawthorne's attempted humor did not quite come off. "You aren't as fast with a gun as you once were, Sam."

The judge gave him a wry grin. "I haven't carried one for nearly ten years."

"And one more man isn't going to mean much, not with the crowd that Duke is apparently bringing in. You sit on the bench and leave the rest to me."

"Creed must have twelve or thirteen men. Deputize them."

Hawthorne hesitated. The judge was impatient.

"So you mistrust his motives. What can he do? He either helps or he doesn't."

The sheriff was not fully convinced. He said as much as he and Reese left the courthouse a few minutes later and walked uptown together.

"I can't figure Ben Creed. I've known him since I first came into this country. I've always found him fair but never knew him to go out of his way to help anyone before. The man's a cold fish."

Reese offered no comment, since his own

feeling about Creed was almost exactly that of the older man.

Hawthorne went on, "Could he be currying favor with Jenny?"

Carstairs glanced at him sharply, but the sheriff's eyes seemed to be caught on the dusty street ahead where two dogs had started a fight.

"What makes you think I'd know about that?"

Hawthorne turned his hard, direct gaze on Reese. "I know that girl pretty well. For a while I figured maybe she would marry Ben. I don't think she will now, not since you came." He walked on, his hands in his pockets as if he had forgotten Reese's existence.

They reached the hotel and went in. Creed was in the lobby with Jenny. They had been standing facing each other across the high desk and whatever their conversation, it must have been intimate for they broke off as they heard the men come through the doorway.

Reese knew a sudden pang of jealousy and had he been alone would have continued across the lobby and up the stairs, but the sheriff walked to the desk, pausing before Creed.

"Reese tells me you've offered to help."

Creed glanced momentarily at Carstairs, then back to the sheriff. "That's right." There was a tiny smile twisting his straight-lipped mouth as if he were daring Hawthorne to question his motives.

Instead Hawthorne said, "I suppose you know that Borden is bringing in gunmen from outside."

"So I've heard."

"How many men are you carrying on your crew?"

"Twenty-one with Davis."

Hawthorne was startled. That was a large crew. A thought struck him. "You added any new ones recently?"

Creed was smiling even more broadly. "Some — right after you served the injunction."

Hawthorne hesitated. Obviously Creed had anticipated the situation and started preparing for it, meaning to turn it to his own advantage. How? Taking a gamble that Reese would be killed in the inevitable gun battle and at the very least impressing Jenny by exposing himself to the same chance on Reese's behalf?

Hawthorne looked at the girl, saw the gratitude in her dark eyes as they rested on Creed. There was a certain savage protest in him and he realized he did not want her to have anything to do with Ben.

He had never analyzed his feelings for Jenny. He was old enough to be her father but the protective tenderness he had for her was more like affection he might have lavished on the wife he never had.

He said to Creed, "I'm going to make you a special deputy and deputize your men, but I expect you to take orders from me, exactly as I expect Reese Carstairs to take orders from me. You will serve the law, not yourselves." It was a challenge.

Creed made no attempt to hide his amusement. He was in the saddle and he knew it and knew Hawthorne knew it. Without his crew no one in the valley could stop Duke Borden from taking the Triple X cattle anywhere that he chose.

"Of course, Sheriff. I'd take orders from you even if I were not deputized. What is it you want?"

"Lend me enough men to ride out and arrest Duke the moment he moves his cattle."

"You'll never arrest him."

Hawthorne was aware of this but stubbornly meant to follow the letter of the law.

"What would you do?"

"Hit them now, before they expect you. Bring Borden in, lock him up and hold him until Reese gets his papers from Texas."

"We can't. We know what he's planning, he's made no bones about it but technically he has not violated the court order until he moves the cattle off his own range."

Creed's smile was gone and the slightest edge of contempt had crept into his voice. "That's the trouble with the law, the weakness of our whole system. It's like giving a rattlesnake the first bite. We can know a man is a criminal, that he plans on breaking a law, but we have to wait until the act is accomplished before we hit him."

The sheriff shrugged. "I didn't make the law, I try to uphold it. It's been developed by a lot of people over a long period."

Creed dropped his mask of patience. "A man protects himself in this world, Hawthorne. You can't run for a man with a star every time you need your nose wiped. You asked me what I'd do. I told you. It's your problem — give the orders and I'll try to follow them. But if some of us get killed, don't blame me. Do you want me to send word to the ranch for men or do you want to ride out there?"

"We'll ride out. We'll work from there. Borden has to drive across your range either way he chooses to go."

Jenny, who had been watching Creed, turned to look at Reese Carstairs. His full attention was on Ben Creed and his face had a drawn, set look as if he were having an inner struggle with himself.

Hawthorne said, "I'll get some things together and be ready to ride in half an hour."

He went out. Reese Carstairs watched him go and turned back, badly wanting a minute alone with the girl. But Creed was there, bold, immobile between them, his presence effectively blocking the words that were crowding to his lips.

He said only, "I'll get my gear," and moved to the stairs, conscious of their eyes on him.

In Jenny's sitting room, Joe Blunt, Bo Martin, and Austin were playing poker, disinterestedly, having no money to risk on the game.

They glanced up as he came in. Bo Martin's dark, narrow face was devoid of expression. He had offered no comment when he heard of his brother's death. He had not mentioned Gil since but Carstairs knew that the bond between the brothers had been close knit, that they could not have thought, or acted, or been more nearly one if they had been twins.

He said, calmly, "We're riding out to Creed's place. The sheriff has deputized all of his crew. Which one of you is going to Denver to meet Pop?"

They hesitated, none wanting to leave. It was Blunt who spoke, feeling more free to offer advice. "He'll be all right. Duke won't be bothering about the papers now."

"One of you goes." It was an order. "I'm going to make sure Pop will be all right."

He advanced to the small table and gathered up the cards, riffling them quickly with his strong fingers. Then he placed the pack face down in the center of the table.

"High card stays. The rest of us ride in half an hour."

He went through the connecting door to Whitey.

A night lamp burned with a small flame on the table beside the bed and in its flickering light Whitey's face looked pale and waxlike. His breathing was shallow and Reese Carstairs hated to wake him but knew Whitey would never forgive him if he rode out without saying good-by.

A gentle hand on the bony shoulder roused the man on the bed, the eyes came open and stared for a full minute of noncomprehension before he oriented himself.

Whitey's voice had the uncertainty of weakness, but his lips curved a little as he recognized Reese.

"Hi, Captain. What's up?"

Reese had reached over and closed his hand on the slim fingers.

"Time to ride. Duke's about ready to start his drive."

There was the shadow of frustration in the other's eyes and Reese knew what was passing through his mind, that this was one of the few times that Reese had ridden into a fight without Whitey beside him.

He said, "The boys are drawing lots to see who goes to Denver to meet Pop. Duke isn't above covering that angle even when he's moving out the cattle. If he could keep us occupied and get to Pop and the papers . . ." He let his voice trail off, noting Whitey's struggle to keep his eyes open. He stood quietly, his touch still light on the other's hand and Whitey's shallow breathing took up the rhythmic evenness of sleep again.

He moved noiselessly out of the room. Joe Blunt was standing beside the card table, holding an ace of spades in hand, his face dark and sullen.

"I'm it." He threw the offending card on the table as if the bit of pasteboard was to blame.

Carstairs winced a little. He understood Blunt so very thoroughly. He understood them all as he understood himself. But none of this showed in his voice as he gave his instructions.

"Go to Denver. Wait at the Hoffman House. Pop will contact you there. Don't use the main road into Walden, cut off and come in through the hills.

"Bo, Austin, get your gear and saddle the horses."

He hesitated a moment, then did something which he had not done during their long association. He put his arm around Blunt's thick shoulders, his fingers digging into the upper arm.

"I'm depending on you, Joe."

He swung quickly away then, half-ashamed of the surge of feeling that rose through him, for if he would miss Whitey riding into a fight, he would miss Joe Blunt more. There was not as much personal feeling but he relied on Joe Blunt's steadiness, his unexcited calculations. He would have far rather had him than Austin, but the cards had made the choice.

He got his things from his room and came down into the lobby to find Creed still beside the desk.

The man turned around slowly. "Ready?"

"In a minute." Carstairs' voice was tight. "I'd like a word alone with Jenny."

For an instant their eyes locked and Reese thought that Creed would refuse. Then surprisingly the man smiled and said in an easy voice, "Of course," and walked alone into the night.

Reese stared after him, aware of some change here which he could not evaluate.

Jenny saw the look. She reached across the desk and put a small hand on his arm. "I told him."

He swung on her. "Told him what?"

"That I couldn't marry him, no matter what happened."

Reese found no words.

"He asked me about you. I said I didn't know. He kissed me — He said he'd take care of you."

Carstairs was around the corner of the desk without knowing how he got there and she was in his arms, her body firm within his grasp, pressing against him as she lifted her mouth to meet his hungry kiss.

SIXTEEN

Ben Creed's ranch had the feel of an army camp. The men who thronged the hard-baked yard were tense, watchful as any soldiers awaiting attack.

Creed made no attempt to carry out the everyday chores which usually occupied the crew. Instead he held the main body of his forces at the ranch, making it headquarters. At Hawthorne's order a half-dozen riders had scattered through the hills watching Borden's men work across the valley floor, pushing the small gathers into the growing herd.

The sheriff sat on the gallery steps, his head bare to the late-afternoon sun, the stubby pipe clenched between his lips. The pipe was out, but the rancid, acrid odor of the damp heel carried to Reese Carstairs who stood leaning against the squared post at the side of the steps and the pipe made a wet wheezing sound rasping his nerves.

He said tensely, "Put it in your pocket."

Hawthorne lifted wise eyes to the younger man's face. "Take it a little easy."

Reese Carstairs returned the look and Hawthorne sensed a wildness in him which he had never observed before. And his voice when he spoke was low, too controlled, as if he held himself in check with effort.

"Seems some of us always have to go a little easy, ride herd on ourselves and our wants while others do anything they damn well please."

Hawthorne had not put away the dead pipe. It hissed louder as he sucked harder on the chewed stem.

"Responsibility, I guess. Some of us have it, others never do. You apparently had to develop it early. Maybe you're naturally that way."

"No!" The word almost burst from Reese in protest, surprising even him. "I never wanted responsibility for others. When they made me a lieutenant I tried to get out of it. I only took the next promotion because I knew by then that men would follow me. Being an officer tied my hands. My impulse was to ride out and fight the Union Army by myself. Right now my impulse is to ride out and kill Duke Borden before a lot of people get hurt."

"But you can't." The sheriff's voice was curiously gentle. "You owe a responsibility to someone else."

"Who?"

"Jenny."

The word seemed to hang in the warm air between them. The cook appeared in the doorway of his shack. The iron rod rattled around the inside rim of the metal triangle, sending its call across the yard.

Ben Creed came from the blacksmith shop with Clem Davis at his side. The men who had been loafing in the shade moved toward the lower end of the yard and Bo Martin and Austin, who had been sitting at the end of the porch rose, looking inquiringly at Reese.

He nodded almost imperceptibly and they headed toward the crowd which was gathering for this early evening meal. The sheriff had made no effort to rise. His eyes were across the yard, on Creed, speculative, thoughtful.

"I still don't trust him."

Carstairs did not answer. For two days he had watched Ben Creed and had found nothing suspicious in his actions. The man had co-operated in every way. He had listened to the sheriff. He had had his scouts report directly to Hawthorne. He had kept in the background, making no suggestions until his opinion had been asked.

He said, "Give him the benefit of the doubt."

Hawthorne shrugged. He rose. He knocked the pipe out against the heel of his hand. He said in a neutral voice, "Let's eat," and led the way down across the yard.

They were half through the meal when Pete Mullins came in. He rode up to the cookshack door. There were too many of them to sit at the long table and they squatted on the ground, holding their tin plates in their hands. Pete came over to where Hawthorne sat beside Reese Carstairs.

"They're moving out."

Hawthorne looked up in surprise. Unconsciously he squinted toward the west where the sun was almost down behind the ragged mountain peaks.

"A night drive."

This he had not expected, for the passes through which Borden must travel were treacherous and narrow. Still, Duke was facing some twenty-five men lined up to keep him from moving the Triple X herd. If he could drive by night, if he could slip by them . . .

Hawthorne felt every eye upon him. He said, "Finish your meal. It may be a long spell before you have time for another."

He rose, motioning Creed and Carstairs to follow him, and moved away from the circle of eating men.

He faced them solidly, steel in his old eyes.

"You're both under orders. Let's don't forget that."

Neither of them answered.

"We'll take the full crew and we're going through to Borden."

"You'll never get through." It was Creed.

Hawthorne's jaw was set stubbornly. "We'll get through. He may have more men than we have, but don't forget he has the herd to worry about. Some of his riders have to stay with the cattle."

Creed's shrug was expressive. Reese Carstairs still did not speak. The sheriff hesitated for an instant, then walked toward the corral.

Within twenty minutes they rode, mounting the low ridge which Creed had always considered as the southern boundary of his range, reaching its top and pausing. The twilight had thickened but there was still enough light for Reese to see the faces of the men around him.

Martin and Austin were at his side protectively, drawn close by the feeling that even though the riders with them were on the same mission there was no real community of interest.

Hawthorne started down the ridge, the others following and suddenly a rifle cracked ahead of them to send its warning out through the night. Hawthorne did not stop.

Ahead of them a creek wound its way across the flattening valley floor, its banks hedged with a thick wall of trees and low-growing brush. The firing came from the shelter of the trees.

A second rifle spoke, this time the bullet

digging into the turf some thirty feet in front of Hawthorne's horse.

He hauled up and the men behind him pulled to a stop, and Duke Borden's voice reached out from the green shelter along the creek.

"Go back, old man. I've got twenty rifles on you."

Hawthorne's voice was clear and unshaken. "You haven't got a chance, Duke. You'll never get those cattle through."

Reese Carstairs was staring above the trees at the valley beyond. In the gathering darkness it was hard to be sure, but it seemed that there was a bunched herd a good mile back. Creed had pulled up at his side, between him and Martin, and Reese wondered aloud, "Am I seeing things, or is that the herd?"

Creed squinted into the distance. "Looks like it. Looks like they haven't started to drive yet."

Hawthorne was again riding forward, slowly this time, the rest not following. "I'm coming in, Duke."

He had covered some fifty feet when far off to Carstairs' right a rifle spat from the ridge top. Reese swore, one of their own men gone trigger-happy. A dozen guns answered from along the creek.

The sheriff, trying to swing his horse, never brought the animal full around. The bullet caught him in the side, flung him from the saddle, and his body jumped twice after it hit the ground as two more heavy-caliber slugs tore their way through him.

Instinctively Carstairs started his horse forward but Austin caught his bridle, holding him. Creed and Bo Martin were already riding for the shelter of the ridge crest and they followed. A horse went down on their left. The man lit running, another went down and he saw Pete Mullins fall heavily. Then they had the crest between them and the creek and Creed had hauled up and was rallying his men.

He turned as Carstairs rode to his side, saying tensely, "Are you taking over or am I?"

"You," said Carstairs. "You know the country and the men."

"All right." Creed's voice tightened. All the impatience had gone, blanketed by a cold reserve of command as if he had been waiting for this moment.

"Borden's got his men bunched along the creek. He figured we'd come this way, but he can't be spread out too far."

He singled out a half-dozen riders.

"Get off your horses, get back to the top of the ridge and keep raking that brush with your guns." He glanced back at Carstairs. "You take half the riders, swing east toward the trail. The brush thins out about a mile downstream. Circle and come at the herd. I'll take the rest and do the same from the opposite direction."

Carstairs nodded. He sat quiet in the saddle, flanked by Martin and Austin, while Creed chose the men, then they were riding along the northern breast of the ridge while behind them the guns of their rear guard hammered at the timber-lined creek.

The ridge lessened, flattening out as they approached the dust ribbon which was the trail, and they swung right, splashing across the creek which here ran between grassed banks with only a scraggle of brush.

It was nearly dark. To their right the spasmodic sound of firing still split the night from the direction of the ridge top and Carstairs hauled up, listening, trying to detect other noise which would indicate that Creed had run into trouble. There was none.

They rode on toward the spot where he had seen the gathered herd and came upon it suddenly. The stock started struggling to its feet in quick alarm.

Carstairs shouted the order to halt, sensing that something was very wrong, not knowing what it was. There were no guards with the herd, and it had been bedded in a wide circle. Certainly Duke Borden had not planned to move it this night.

The cattle started milling slowly, uncertain, gripped by the nervousness which transmits itself through bunched animals like an electric spark.

And then he heard the sound of running horses and guessed that it might be Creed and called a warning to come in carefully.

Creed's answer was clear in the thin air and Reese rode gingerly around the restless animals to meet him.

The rancher was as jumpy as he was. "What goes on? What's Duke up to now?"

Carstairs did not know. "Any trouble?"

"None." Creed held up his hand. "Listen."

They sat in silence, the stillness of the night broken only by the pawing of the shifting, uneasy herd.

"It doesn't make sense." Creed sounded irritated. He was not a man who liked puzzles, who liked things he did not understand. He leaned lightly into the stirrups and guided his horse into the press of cattle.

"There's a lot of calves and she-stock." His voice came back above the sound of lowing.

Carstairs caught his meaning, that Duke had cut out the marketable steers and left the culls and she-stock as a decoy.

"But there are steers." His quick eye had singled out the beef animals.

Reese moved in, the pack giving grudgingly before his horse. These animals were not the half wild, gaunted cattle of the southern plains. They showed the mark of good graze, plenty of water, close to the home ranch.

A match flared in Creed's hand and Carstairs heard his muttered curse.

"What's the matter now?"

"This steer. It's got my brand, and this one and this, and this . . ." His voice rose as his anger grew.

"You know what he's done? He's left the Triple X she-stuff and calves and any steers of mine which were mixed up with his, as a decoy."

"But where's the main herd?"

Creed pushed through to rejoin Carstairs. "They can't have gone up Kings Canyon. They would have had to pass too close to my place and my scouts would have spotted them. He's probably been moving them up through the timber along the west bench in small bunches. They're undoubtedly in the Platte valley heading for the old Indian Encampment."

Carstairs stared at him.

"The smart bastard." It was Creed. "The canny bastard. I didn't give him credit for this much sense. He purposely gathered these, out in the open where my men could see them, while the other members of his crew worked the shipping stock north.

"Then he lined up along the creek to make us fight our way through. I'll bet the men in the trees have gone. They'll throw a rear guard across the Platte valley and try to hold us. If we do break through, if we succeed in stampeding the cattle they'll only run up the valley in the way that Duke wants them to go. It looks as if he's won this hand. Let's see if we can take the final one."

SEVENTEEN

When Hawthorne fell Duke Borden cursed savagely. It was not that he felt any real sorrow for the sheriff's death. Human life, except for his own, meant little to him. And he had expected men would die in the upshaping battle, but it was one thing for a man to be killed in the hot surge of a running fight and something else to shoot down a law officer in the pursuit of his duty.

He had not planned coming back into this territory. Until this moment he had figured to buy another ranch, build it into a spread greater than the Triple X. Now he realized that once the cattle were sold he would have to change his name and lose himself in the rough country to the west. A hunted man cannot afford to be tied down.

He watched Creed's men gain the safety of the ridge top. He wished that some of the bullets which his men threw against the hillside had found Reese Carstairs and Creed, but that had been almost too much to expect.

Aside from the shooting-down of Hawthorne, things were working for him according to schedule and he grinned in the darkness, visualizing what was happening behind the lodge. If they had seen it, and he was almost certain that they had, they would already be circling to reach the bedded herd.

He called to Mart January, "Time to pull out. Leave three men. Tell them to keep pounding at the ridge for fifteen minutes and then drift."

He moved to his horse, picketed at the edge of the brush. Firing started suddenly from the ridge top and a bullet tore through the undergrowth not half a dozen feet from where he was untying his big gray. He cursed, swinging into the saddle and calling sharply to the men.

He led the way quickly along the creek. Behind him a man went down, his horse shying away. Borden did not even look back.

They were out of the line of fire from the ridge when he checked the pace, going forward cautiously, as soundlessly as possible. He heard Creed's men ahead and stopped, motioning the others behind him into the shelter of the brush. They stayed still, listening, as the BC crew swept past heading for the decoy herd.

When they were safely gone, Duke spurred his horse into a run, leading the way to the Platte and the valley beyond. He had achieved what he set out to do, gotten the herd up the Platte valley without being observed and he and the main crew were now between Creed, Carstairs, and the driven stock.

He was sure he had more men, enough to fight a rear-guard action while the rest pushed the cattle northward.

On an ordinary drive five to ten miles a day would be considered good progress, but he only had fifty miles to go. There was plenty of water and the animals were butter-fat, could stand being hurried.

At the valley's narrow neck, where hills like guardian bastions thrust out from the mountain's flank to nearly block the passage of the swift stream, he meant to make his stand and he gave curt orders to January.

"Have the men fan out. Let Creed's crew ride halfway in before you start shooting. I'll be back."

January eyed him. "Where you going?"

"To make sure everything's all right with the drive."

The moon had come up into the eastern sky, still low, but it gave enough light to show Borden January's dissatisfied expression.

"You don't like it?"

January said, "No." He said it carefully as if he measured each word before it passed his lips. "You can send someone else. This is your fight. You should be here."

Impatience and anger rode up through Borden, but he curbed the words which sprang to his lips. He needed January. The trouble was he did not trust the man. Still, January's whole future was linked with his.

He said calmly, "All right. You want to ride so badly. Ride. Tell the boys with the herd to keep them moving no matter what happens. If Creed's men break through, they're to stampede them. The stock will have to run up the valley, there isn't much else they can do."

January looked at him oddly. Then with a shrug, roweled his horse forward. Borden turned to his men. There were twenty of them. He had left three beside the creek to cover their retreat and there were six with the drive.

He had them dismount, two of them lead all the horses into a rocky draw on the right where they would be out of the way of chance bullets, yet handy enough if they were forced to pull out in a hurry. He placed the men with care.

It was a natural trap, and unless Creed and Carstairs were fools which he did not believe for a moment, they would know it. But he did not care whether they rode into it. His main idea was delay.

He sat down finally, his rifle across his thick knees, and lighted a cigarette. His shirt was damp with sweat, and he suddenly felt how much the nervous strain was telling on him.

He waited. He heard the men shifting around in the rocks above him. He listened, his ears reaching for sounds from the trail. The moon had climbed into the sky, a yellow disk, looking enormous, so close that it could almost be touched.

He had no interest in it save for the light it threw, and then there were horses coming and he was at once alert, calling a low-voiced warning to his men. He was standing, having no memory of coming to his feet. His rifle was gripped in his hands and then he realized there were only two or three horses on the trail and remembered the men he had left in the brush along the creek.

He called to the others to hold their fire, studying the men as they rode into the pass, trying to recognize them in the uncertain light.

Suddenly he was sure, and shouted. They pulled up and a voice carried back, "Borden?"

"That's right."

The man was nervous. "They aren't too far behind us."

"Okay. Get your horses up the draw." He watched them as they obeyed, turning up the rocky side canyon toward the picketing spot. They came at a shuffling run back to Borden.

"Any trouble?" he asked.

"No. But Collins is dead."

Collins was the man whose horse had gone down behind Borden. Duke showed no interest. He assigned each to a spot in the rocks.

"Don't shoot until you hear my gun. I'd like to suck them clear into the pass."

He returned to his place. Waiting was always the hardest chore, and it seemed to him that he had spent most of his life in waiting, first for Nell to marry Reese, then for a safe opportunity to get rid of Alf and take the ranch. He heard the hoofbeats and was again on his feet, standing behind his sheltering boulder, his big form seeming to blend into the shadow of the timber which grew down the steep slope behind him.

His eyes stung from trying to see, the sharp salt taste of excitement was in his mouth, the waiting was nearly over.

Ben Creed knew every foot of the ground over which he and Carstairs traveled and he had already decided that Duke Borden would make a stand in the pass ahead. It was the logical place. But he said nothing to the man at his side.

Carstairs noted the jutting hills which seemed to fold in on them, the turn of the trail ahead as it swung to pass between the jawlike banks. He expected Creed to call a halt, not wanting to take over command himself, yet warned by the sixth sense of danger which a trained soldier develops.

Creed plunged ahead. Carstairs glanced around to where Bo Martin, Austin, and Clem Davis rode at his flank.

There were no signs of guards as they came into the pass and he began to relax a little. Then, without warning, Creed slashed his heavy quirt across the flank of Carstairs' horse, the beaded end laying open the rump flesh.

The startled animal leaped forward. Behind him Carstairs heard Bo Martin's curse but did not see the Cajun drive his horse at Creed. The rancher pivoted and Clem Davis bludgeoned Bo from the saddle with his rifle barrel.

Austin spurred after his captain and was at his side as Carstairs fought to bring his frightened mount under control. They swept around the curve together and Duke Borden fired, his shot a signal which turned loose twenty guns.

Borden's bullet struck Carstairs' horse, it stumbled, plunged headlong, throwing Reese over the rocks to drop across the edge of the rushing stream.

He fell, not into the churning water but onto a small spit of sand built up in the eddy caused by two high boulders, and lay there for a full minute, the wind knocked out of him.

Austin had gone down under the first withering blast, a bullet through his neck, another through his head.

Duke Borden was trying to spot Carstairs' body in the bad light and the screen of dust raised by the horse. He had expected a full crew to ride in, not merely two men. He was certain Reese had been in the lead and Reese had disappeared.

Cautiously he came from his hiding place and advanced down over the rocks, calling to his men to cover him. Carstairs saw him coming. He was on his knees, peering out between the boulders which marked the edge of the creek bed. He resisted the impulse to send a bullet crashing into Borden's thick body, knowing the shot would bring down a murderous fire from above.

And the instinct to live was strong within him. He ducked back, crawling painfully along the wet sand into a niche which was hardly large enough for his body. He crouched there, holding his breath, the spray from the dashing creek riding over him in a fine mist.

He heard the grate of Borden's boots and heard the man's grunt as he paused beside Carstairs' dead horse. The horse had veered away after throwing its rider and lay in a twisted heap some ten yards from the stream.

Borden looked toward the bank and came forward, his rifle held ready, pausing on the brink to peer down at the white-lashed water.

The moonlight failed to reach into the trough of the creek and he did not see the marks that Carstairs had left on the damp sand.

But he was not satisfied and started down the bank. He had not reached the bottom when the shot whined down from above. He whirled, diving for the mouth of the draw in which the horses were tethered.

The fire from the high timber increased. One of his men was hit, a second and then a third. They were tumbling after him and as they ran Ben Creed, at the head of his remaining crew, came through the gap. Creed had sent a half-dozen men upward to flank the Triple X riders and waited with the rest, screened by the curve in the trail.

Creed had no doubt that Reese Carstairs was dead, but Carstairs' death was not enough. He had no intention of allowing Borden to escape or of having the herd driven clear of the territory. He would complete Reese's mission himself, bring the stock back to Alf Carstairs' son, supply the strength for Jenny to lean on in her grief over Reese Carstairs' death.

Leading the charge, he trapped Borden's men in the draw as they tried to mount, caught in a murderous cross fire from the ridge above and the mounted crew with Creed.

And Duke Borden seemed to lose all reason, spurring his horse directly at Ben Creed. Creed fired twice, seeing the bullets strike home, seeing him come on and then, when less than twenty feet separated them, Borden brought up his Colt and squeezed the trigger.

The pin fell on an empty cartridge. Duke stared at the weapon, unbelieving, in the instant before Creed shot him deliberately through the head.

Duke's men, the few remaining, panicked, swerved as they came out of the draw and headed upvalley, bent low in their saddles, fleeing the driving shots of the BC crew.

One went down, a second, but the rest rounded the far bend and were lost in the night.

Reese saw Creed lead his men in pursuit and they ran up the slanting trail and out of sight.

The canyon was suddenly still after the din of ricocheting sound, silent with the haunted feel of death.

Carstairs crawled from his hiding place and climbed stiffly up the bank. Half a dozen men and horses were scattered along the trail and he moved from one to the other, pausing briefly to make certain that all were dead. Then he turned downward, past Austin's body and found Bo Martin beside the trail.

He bent over the small Cajun and was surprised to find him still breathing. The dark hair was split by an ugly, two-inch red gash on the side of his head. The breathing was labored, very shallow.

He straightened, looking around, hopeful that one of the riderless horses might be close by.

There were none and he stood for a long moment in contemplative thought. He could not leave Bo. Creed's crew might return at any time and it was obvious Creed had meant him to be killed in the fight, and that he would not leave a witness like Martin alive.

He stopped. He caught the small body in his arms and climbed toward the sheltering timber. Not until he found a place behind some rocks where the ground leveled into a small cup did he pause for breath.

Martin's breathing was weaker. He felt the wrist and found the irregular pulse. The man, he knew, was going to die. He stood up, knowing a savage helplessness, a need to do something, anything. There were only four of them left: Joe Blunt, Pop Greer, Whitey Ellis, and himself.

Torn by indecision, he looked out across the valley. Far off to the east a widening band of light told him it would soon be day.

He debated the long walk toward town; it must be a good thirty miles and once in the open he would have no protection, no cover.

It was closer to Creed's ranch, not over ten miles at the most, but he had no idea what reception he would find there, what orders Creed might have given regarding himself.

And he remembered he had dropped his rifle in his fall and started searching for another. Bo Martin's was lying beside the trail below him. He could see it in the growing morning light. He was halfway down the slope when he heard the beat of hoofs and stopped.

He returned to Bo Martin on a lurching run and found the Raider dead and crouched beside the still form, unholstering his sidearm.

EIGHTEEN

Creed's men caught the slowly moving herd less than five miles above the pass, but there was almost no fight. The Triple X crew fleeing uptrail had met January coming and told the foreman what had happened.

January had ridden back with them, giving his orders quickly, realist enough to know that with Borden dead the game was over. Even if the remaining riders could stand off Creed's men they could not sell the herd.

He called the drovers together, telling them briefly that he was riding north and they had best follow. There was no argument. For most of them this was not the first time to fade into the hills leaving no trail behind.

Had Creed's men been ten minutes later they would have experienced no opposition at all. As it was, only a few scattered shots greeted their approach as they rode warily in, then the last of Borden's men pulled out, heading across the sweeping valley for the timber and safety.

Creed made no effort at pursuit. He understood exactly what was in January's mind and in the minds of those who followed him.

The cattle were too tired from the hard night drive to stampede easily. They churned in nervousness at the rattle of shots, but did not run.

Creed had hauled up and was talking to Davis, his men around him. He sat looking at the herd which had caused so much trouble, so many deaths.

"Turn 'em around and head 'em back. Once they're in the Park, let 'em scatter."

Creed had not worked out the details but he meant to make some arrangement with Nell for peace with the Triple X, knowing he held the bargaining position but still viewing his own actions with Jenny's eyes.

To Davis, he said, "Let's go find Carstairs' body. Too bad he didn't live to see his herd come home."

Clem Davis gave him a small, tight-lipped grin. "Too bad," he agreed, understanding Creed thoroughly.

They returned downtrail and came around the upper curve and into the pass in silence.

"There's Carstairs' horse." He pulled up beside it, staring down at the dead animal. "But where is he?"

Creed's voice had tightened, as the possibility dawned on him that Reese Carstairs might be alive. He cursed himself, knowing he should have stopped to check before riding after Borden's men.

He stepped down, handing the bridle to Clem Davis, and quartered across the flinty soil until he came to the creek's edge. Standing there he looked down on the bar of damp sand.

The depression where Reese's shoulder had struck still showed, partly filled with the seeping water. The marks of his hands and knees were plain and the trampled condition of the sand between the rocks showed where he had crouched.

Ben Creed looked up quickly, caution upon him as his eyes climbed the rising mountainside. If Carstairs was hiding there, armed with a rifle, both he and Davis were in danger. But nothing moved and he went back to Carstairs' horse, noting that the rifle was still in the boot beneath the saddle fender.

This did not mean much, since every man in both parties had carried rifles and the dead men had no need for theirs. Methodically he walked from one corpse to the next, pausing to make certain that each was dead, accounting for the rifles.

Davis watched him, slumped a little tiredly in the saddle. "What's the matter?"

"Carstairs is alive somewhere."

"Maybe he got a horse and took out."

"Maybe." Creed did not sound convinced. He took his horse's bridle and led it forward toward the lower bend, careful to keep it between himself and the slope on his right.

Davis, an old hand himself, swung out of the saddle and followed suit.

They reached the curve and rounded it and stopped. Creed was staring at a black spot in the dust where blood had oxidized to a hardened lump.

"Isn't this about where you knocked Martin out of the saddle?"

Davis grunted his assent.

"Where is he?"

"Maybe he got up and walked away, although I'd have sworn he'd never walk again."

Creed's eyes were on the trail between them and the mountainside. He found another spot of dried blood, this one hardly larger than a dime. He moved forward following the signs upward across the broken rocks, losing them, finding them again, always climbing.

Davis had left the horses to join him, his rifle carried ready in the crook of his left arm.

From high above Reese Carstairs watched them. It was too far for a revolver shot. It would be sheer accident if he hit them from this distance.

They reached the edge of trees and disappeared into them, and Carstairs knew that the hunt was on in earnest, that Ben Creed would do everything in his power to keep him from leaving the mountain slope alive.

His mouth set grimly. There were two of them, and they had rifles, but in the thick timber and upthrust rocks the longer guns were a doubtful advantage. He worked higher, hunting a place to hide, a place to lie in wait.

He heard them when they discovered Ben's body, their voices carrying to him.

The sun stood in the eastern sky, but its slanting rays did not reach deep into the wooded hills and the mountain air had the crisp chill of early dawn.

Carstairs shivered; his blood was still thin from years in the warmer climate of Mexico. Moving swiftly, he came suddenly to the timberline, and stared unbelievingly at the rock dike which rose before him, a granite upthrust which was the crest of the mountain itself.

It was totally unexpected. Until now the climb had been surprisingly easy. He stared at the wall which towered several hundred nearly perpendicular feet toward the arched sky. Passage over it would be treacherous and even if he succeeded in working his way up one of the narrow crevices which marred the face, he would be a perfect target.

He cursed softly to himself, this came of not knowing the country. He was trapped, he could only go downward.

He moved cautiously, searching each small

clearing before he stepped into it, and suddenly caught movement in the trees to his right and froze.

The man was lost in the thick foliage of the pines, and then he had another glimpse and snapped a quick shot.

The answering cry was sharp and filled with shock. Clem Davis staggered into view, taking three reeling steps before falling forward to lie quiet on his face.

But Reese hardly saw him, for a rifle had begun to spit from his left in a studied pattern as Creed shifted his aim a foot at a time, hoping to cut his unseen adversary down.

Reese dropped, holding his fire, his revolver not a match for the rifle, not wanting to expose his position accurately. He worked forward on his knees and elbows while the rifle bullets continued their search above him. Suddenly the firing stopped and Creed's voice reached out to him, uncontrolled, violent.

"Come on out and let's finish it."

Reese thought the rancher hoped to track him by the sound of his voice. He remained silent, shifting noiselessly. He meant to live, to have Jenny and build the life he had ridden out of Mexico to find.

A stone rolled under his boot heel and went bounding down the mountainside, careening from one tree trunk to the next until it was lost in the canyon below.

This time it was the spat of a six-gun, not the rifle, and Carstairs wondered if the man were out of rifle shells.

He moved on, coming behind a pile of rocks and, rising behind their shelter, decided to work downhill, attempt to reach the horses which Creed had left below. He dared not remain on the mountainside too long and risk the arrival of Creed's crew. The only man he might count on for help, if he were still alive, would be Moose Kobbler. The last he had seen of the storekeeper, the man had been riding in the rear guard.

He came to the edge of a small clearing and suddenly Ben Creed was facing him, gun at the ready. Before Reese could bring his own weapon up, Creed fired, too quickly, the heavy slug striking Reese's gun, tearing it from his grasp to send it spinning into the brush. The impact numbed Reese's hand and arm and instinctively he glanced at his fingers, surprised to find them unharmed.

His eyes fastened on Creed who was walking deliberately forward, a grin twisting his lips. Reese Carstairs had brushed close to death many times but he knew that he had never come closer than he was in this instant. Creed was making sure, with machinelike precision, of this ultimate step in his plan to get Jenny. Carstairs recalled the shot from one of their own men which had precipitated the action resulting in Hawthorne's death and wondered fleetingly if this had been ordered in the hope the answering bullets would also cut him down.

If he turned to run now, Creed would catch him in the back. He preferred to face the man. Creed stopped walking with some fifteen feet separating them. He seemed to be purposely dragging out the time, satisfying some deep, sadistic urge.

Neither spoke and the morning around them was perfectly still. Reese saw the muscles along Creed's jaw tighten and tensed himself for the shock of the bullet. It never came.

Creed's finger tightened on the trigger and the hammer fell on an empty cartridge.

Both men were held in an instant of sharp surprise, then Reese leaped forward with the quick automation of long training, even as Creed fumbled at his belt for fresh shells, and crashed a fist into the man's face.

Creed dropped his gun, staggering backward, off balance. Carstairs' driving shoulder caught him in the side and carried him to the ground.

They rolled over and over in the soft cushion of age-old needles which carpeted the clearing. Carstairs' fingers closed on Creed's throat, but, still numb from the shock of the bullet striking his gun, could not hold and the rancher broke free, lurching to his knees, then his feet. His hand grasped the bone handle of the knife which protruded from his boot and he pulled the broad, eight-inch blade.

Reese caught the glint of the morning sun on the metal's surface and felt for his own knife. It was gone from its sheath, probably lost when he fell from his horse.

Creed's eyes gleamed and he moved in, like a fencer, on balance. Carstairs backed away from the thrusting point of the heavy knife, his eyes watchful, every sense alert, flexing his fingers in an effort to restore full circulation to his gun hand.

His boot heel caught on an exposed root and he stumbled backward. Creed uttered a wordless cry of triumph and was on him with a catlike leap, the knife stabbing out. Reese took the blow on his left arm, using it as a shield, the point digging to jar against the bone. Before Creed could free it Reese grabbed the wrist, lifting it until the heavy blade pulled free.

He was too intent to feel pain from the oozing cut. He now held Creed's forearm with both hands and they stood, close together, straining, Creed to free his wrist, Carstairs twisting it, trying to make him drop the knife. Then Creed hinged backward and Reese fell on top of him, pushing Creed's right hand above his head.

The rancher used his left, battering ineffectually at Carstairs' ribs, gaining nothing and shifting his attack to his opponent's throat, cutting his wind.

Carstairs still gripped the knife arm, but as the pressure on his neck increased his head swam and small black spots danced before his eyes.

In desperation he brought his left hand down, tearing at the smothering grasp, managing to pry up the middle finger, bending it backward until the bone snapped. Creed yelled. The hand fell away and Carstairs almost sobbed as he pumped fresh air into his tortured lungs.

He lacked the strength to hold the wrist, and Creed wrenched it free, bringing the knife around in a slashing cut which laid open Reese's shoulder. He tried another blow, but Reese rolled away and the knife buried itself in the ground as Reese came to his feet.

Creed tried to free it and Reese used the moment to kick him heavily in the side and felt the ribs bend beneath his boot toe. The man groaned, slumping forward, half on his knees, half on his face, still gripping the knife.

Carstairs stepped on the extended wrist with his heel, twisting savagely and at last Creed's grip on the bone handle was broken.

Reese stooped. He had it free of the holding ground when Creed found the strength to grab his leg and dump him. He fell, the hand which held the knife caught beneath him and before he could roll over Creed was on him, his uninjured arm sliding around beneath Carstairs' chin, pulling it up until the neck threatened to crack.

Reese used his last strength to roll, throwing Creed and coming up slowly to his knees. Both were nearly beat. His head was funny, thought difficult, his reactions slow. Through the blanketing fog he knew that he was on his feet, that Creed was up, facing him, charging as if he had lost sanity.

It took real effort to lift the knife as the big man leaped at him, to drive it between the lower ribs, clear to the hilt.

The force of Creed's rush knocked him backward and Creed fell on top of him. He did not know that the man was dead, he only knew that the man's full weight was across him, pinning him to the ground. He tried to roll from under, pushing at the flaccid body with his last remaining strength.

Somehow he managed, crawling upward to his feet, staring at his empty right hand, dazedly puzzled by the absence of the knife. Then slowly he bent, his movements leaden as he turned the rancher over, the bone handle of the knife standing upright from Creed's side.

Reese wiped a hand across his eyes. He stood there, swaying a little, time meaning nothing until his senses partly cleared. Then he glanced around, half-expecting to see other enemies closing in.

There was no one. Automatically he started down the slope toward the trail below, his only thought to reach the horses which Creed had left there. He never remembered clearly how he made the descent, how long it took, or how he managed to drag himself into the saddle. All he knew was that he had mounted, that he turned the horse and headed out of the pass toward the distant town.

He rode slumped forward, almost on the neck, barely holding his place, the horse choosing its own gait. Teetering on the edge of unconsciousness, he was only faintly aware when Moose Kobbler found him.

Kobbler himself had a wounded shoulder, but he knew that Carstairs needed far more help than he did.

NINETEEN

Jenny Borden had slept little since Reese Carstairs and Creed had ridden away with the sheriff. She was in the kitchen when she heard the clamor from the street and Nell came from the lobby to call in excited horror,

"It's Reese. They say he's dead."

Jenny dropped the dish she had been washing, not even hearing the crash of breaking china, and then she was running, past her sister, across the dining room and out through the lobby.

There was a crowd in the center of the street and two tired horses, heads down, standing to one side.

She stopped on the gallery, afraid to go farther, and saw Dr. Dice hurry forward and the crowd part to let him pass and close again after him.

Then Moose Kobbler, blood plastering the shirt to his thick chest, came through the bunched people and walked on uncertain legs to face her.

"Is he alive?" Her voice was a whisper.

Moose nodded. "But bad hurt — been in a knife fight." Behind him four men were carrying Reese toward the hotel, Dr. Dice alongside, calling out to Jenny.

"A bed."

The need for action aroused her. She went ahead of them, leading the way up the stairs and into a room with a freshly made bed.

"Lost a lot of blood," the doctor told her as they worked to strip the clothes from Reese's unconscious body. "Don't know how he stayed in a saddle."

"He's got to live." She had not meant to say the words aloud.

Dr. Dice looked at her. "He'll live," he said positively, "but he isn't going to do much moving around for a spell."

Tears stung her eyes and she grinned crookedly at the doctor.

Moose Kobbler, leaning unnoticed against the wall by the door, said, low-voiced, "You'll want to know. Duke's dead — a lot of them on both sides are dead — the cattle will have to be rounded up."

Nell came through the door with hot water, hearing the storekeeper's words.

"Then we didn't lose." Her voice was shaky with relief. Jenny looked at her sister, not really seeing her, wondering at her own lack of reaction to the news of Duke's death. And then she remembered Creed.

"Ben?" she asked.

From the bed, Reese's voice was weak, but the words were distinct, carefully formed. "He's dead, Jenny. I don't know how it happened."

Jenny and the doctor bent quickly over him but his eyes were closed; he had slipped back into unconsciousness as if the important thing had been said.

Dr. Dice turned to Nell. "Jenny can help me here," he said. "Take Moose somewhere to lie down and start cleaning up that shoulder. I'll be along to take a look at it."

Nell hesitated. The doctor's voice went hard. "There'll be other wounded. I've sent men out to bring them in. Don't waste time."

Nell said briskly, "Of course," and led Moose Kobbler into the hall.

In the next six days a number of things happened and Reese Carstairs heard of them from Jenny who remained in almost constant attendance on him. She allowed herself time away to attend the funeral when Ben Creed was put to rest alongside Duke Borden, Sheriff Hawthorne, and the other dead from both sides.

Judge Burke came to the hotel to see Reese and report that the suddenly shamed inhabitants of the Park had volunteered to round up the cattle, offered help in many various ways.

"You're a hero," he told Carstairs drily.

"And Hawthorne, too." Then earnestly, "He'd be glad to know he made his point. They see it now — it wasn't just you or Duke or the cattle — it was our way of life."

Reese looked at Jenny. She met his eyes and understanding between them needed no words.

Burke was speaking again, "I don't suppose you know, but you inherit the BC ranch, Miss Jenny."

The girl and Reese reacted in amazement, staring at the judge.

"Drew the will myself," he went on, "almost a year ago. Ben had no relatives. He figured on marrying you but he wanted you cared for in any case."

Jenny said, "I don't see how I can take it," and she was asking Reese.

Reese Carstairs took his time in answering, for suddenly he comprehended the driving force of Creed's feeling for the girl and hesitated to sit in judgment on the man's methods.

He was fair-minded enough to wonder, if their positions had been reversed, how far he himself would have been willing to go. And he was glad that he had not told Jenny of Creed's treachery. Some instinct must have prompted him to let her believe Creed had died fighting at his side.

He said, "Take it. It's the nicest thing you could do for Ben."

She reached for his hand. "Thank you for understanding."

She was interrupted as Whitey Ellis appeared in the doorway, his thin face flushed.

"Pop and Joe just rode in from Denver."

Reese relaxed against the supporting pillows, taking a long, slow breath.

The Raiders were home, not all of them, but for those who remained, the trail was ended. It had been a long way back.

ABOUT THE AUTHOR

Todhunter Ballard was born in Cleveland, Ohio. He was graduated with a Bachelor's degree from Wilmington College in Ohio, having majored in mechanical engineering. His early years were spent working as an engineer before he began writing fiction for the magazine market. As W. T. Ballard he was one of the regular contributors to *Black Mask Magazine* along with Dashiell Hammett and Erle Stanley Gardner. Although Ballard published his first Western story in *Cowboy Stories* in 1936, the same year he married Phoebe Dwiggins, it wasn't until *Two-Edged Vengeance* (1951) that he produced his first Western novel. Ballard later claimed that Phoebe, following their marriage, had co-written most of his fiction with him and perhaps this explains, in part, his memorable female characters. Ballard's Golden Age as a Western author came in the 1950s and extended to the early 1970s. *Incident at Sun Mountain* (1952), *West of Quarantine* (1953), and *High Iron* (1953) are among his finest early historical titles, published by Houghton Mifflin. After numerous traditional Westerns for various publishers, Ballard returned to the historical novel in *Gold in California!* (1965) which earned him a Golden Spur Award from the Western Writers of America. It is a story set during the Gold Rush era of the 'Forty-Niners. However, an even more panoramic view of that same era is to be found in Ballard's *magnum opus, The Californian* (1971), with its contrasts between the *Californios* and the emigrant gold-seekers, and the building of a freight line to compete with Wells Fargo. It was in his historical fiction that Ballard made full use of his background in engineering combined with exhaustive historical research. However, these novels are also character-driven, gripping a reader from first page to last with their inherent drama and the spirit of adventure so true of those times.

The employees of Thorndike Press hope you have enjoyed this Large Print book. All our Thorndike and Wheeler Large Print titles are designed for easy reading, and all our books are made to last. Other Thorndike Press Large Print books are available at your library, through selected bookstores, or directly from us.

For information about titles, please call:

(800) 223-1244

or visit our Web site at:

www.gale.com/thorndike
www.gale.com/wheeler

To share your comments, please write:

Publisher
Thorndike Press
295 Kennedy Memorial Drive
Waterville, ME 04901